DARKEST SINNER

THE DARK ONES SAGA 5

BY

#1 *New York Times* Bestselling Author

RACHEL VAN DYKEN

Darkest Sinner
The Dark Ones Saga Book 5
by Rachel Van Dyken

DARKEST SINNER

ISBN: 9781695217171
Cover Art by Jena Brignola
Formatting by Jill Sava, Love Affair With Fiction

THE RULES
OF THE GODS

"No god may be alone with a human woman, it is forbidden."

"A god must at all times be fair."

"A god shall never intervene in the human plane."

"To keep obedience and order within creation—a god is given one soul and will live forever, that is unless he or she gives into their baser instincts and chooses to side with evil. Once the soul gets sick, the god will begin to lose his power. The god will revert to a cursed state and stay there for an eternity."

"A god without a soul is lost, a god without a heart—is without hope."

"A god may travel out of time if he or she chooses, but must never intervene within the human race if they decide to do so. Traveling to the future is allowed once—the god will be trapped in that time for eternity."

PROLOGUE

Egypt 985 BC

My eyes were not the same.

My body was heavy.

Everything was wrong, something had happened. I stared down at my shaking hands.

I caught her svelte movement first.

I was in the presence of power.

And for the first time in my existence, her smile made me feel like I had a soul, for seconds, in that stare from the goddess's eyes as she moved toward me—I was alive.

Why was I here? Did I do this?

Who are you? My blood pulsed and then settled into a dull roar beneath my skin. This was wrong. Wasn't it?

I breathed in the scent of wildflowers and pine as she moved through the pyramid, her silk robes rustled across the pebbles.

Fire erupted through the torches lining the walls. Light swirled beneath her olive skin as she held up her hand. And in her palm.

A seed.

One small seed.

She waved her hand in front of my face and then opened her palm, the seed had pressed itself into her skin. I watched in awe as its branches wrapped around her arm like tight bracelets, only to stop when they reached her shoulder.

"Ask me." Her voice boomed.

I was on holy ground.

I should be struck down.

Demons were not allowed in the temple.

It was a risk I was willing to take.

For years I had wandered in that desert, forgetting who I was, what I was, cursed to crawl across the hot sand in search of salvation.

Cursed to rule a race that wanted nothing to do with me, but there was a before, wasn't there? I just didn't know who that person was, and I would die to find out.

Sell my very body.

I would rather be struck dead by the Creator than live another day with the burn on my flesh, the need to consume other humans in order to survive, the lust I felt during, the shame that happened after.

I was of the first made.

I was the last of the first left.

And I was alone.

A man alone is a terrible thing.

A demon alone is a dangerous thing.

But a soulless demon alone?

That is a tragedy.

It is worse than death.

I was weak from needing to feed.

I was tired from my two-day trek.

And I was thirsty for a life I knew I would never have unless I took it for myself. I wanted to be reinstated to before, even if it meant I was worse off than I was now, covered in dust.

"Ask me." Fire lit in her irises as the branches from beneath her skin began piercing through toward me, pulling me close, wrapping me tight.

This is how I would die.

I saw it in her eyes.

Dark kohl bled like tear drops from the corner of each fire-lit eye. She did not blink, she stared through me.

She would see no soul.

She would know my shame.

She would know I was the last of the first.

She would know.

I didn't move.

Let her see.

Let her know.

The branches squeezed around my arms, pinning them to my sides as she watched.

"Ask. Me."

My lungs burned as I screeched out. "More."

"More what?" Her head tilted from the left to the right like she was bouncing the idea around.

"More." I gritted my teeth. "More than this."

"You think you deserve more after the things you have done?"

"Quite the opposite." Her grip lessened on my body allowing me more air. "I deserve less—but I want more."

"You know what you are asking." She did not release me, but at least she wasn't squeezing my lungs into tiny pieces of kindling. "Only the Creator has the power to give you more, to restore you. And even then—I cannot give you a good soul."

"So it's useless," I whispered.

She grinned. "I said I cannot give you a good soul—but it is possible to give you one that has been… used."

"I want it."

"You want what you do not understand," she snapped.

"Anything," My body started to shake; already I was too weak from her presence. Food. I needed food. "I will not survive this—and I will not take my life like the others before me."

"You may as well take your own life with what I see in your future." She laughed, it sounded like screams from the depths of Tartarus. I couldn't cover my ears. So I waited for her enjoyment to cease.

"What will you give me for this used soul, Demon?"

"What do you want?"

Her smile was cruel. "Entertainment."

"I must be misunderstanding you."

"I will be watching," she said cryptically. "For now, take your used soul, and feed."

The fires roared around me as the branches broke off and fell to the ground. The goddess was gone.

The body remained.

"Help!" The human girl reached for me. "I do not know where I am. I need—" She shook her head as blood dripped down her arm.

The goddess had left the body.

But the scars from the seed remained.

I watched in horror as her body began to convulse, the veins in her arms flashed blue—then black.

"Feed." A voice carried across the wind.

My mouth was on her neck before I could process the thought, I drank deep, and when I felt her life leave, I sucked the remaining parts of her soul and kept them for myself.

I saw her fears.

I saw myself the way she saw me.

A monster.

And before my very eyes, I became exactly what I always feared I would become.

Powerful beyond all measure.

And trapped for an eternity in a man's body I did not choose, with memories of people's deaths of which I was the cause.

My hell was not death.

My hell.

Was life.

CHAPTER ONE

TIMBER

Present Day, Seattle

The Strange Case of Dr. Jekyll and Mr. Hyde—one of the most realistic books ever written. It may as well be an autobiography. I scratched my nails across the seed tattoo in the middle of my palm and winced when it pulsed back at me.

It had a heartbeat.

Two days ago, it started itching.

Two days ago, I dreamed of the goddess who cursed me.

Two days ago, I saw the goddess who had sworn to love me forever only to go back on her promise the minute the goddesses of earth were welcomed back into the realm.

It was coincidence.

It was concerning.

"Stop fidgeting." Mason my prickly werewolf colleague—he'd rather die than consider me a friend—was currently trying to cut it from my skin, and doing a shit job at it. "I think I have it."

His nail dug into my palm deep.

So deep I had to grit my teeth. I knew it wouldn't kill me, it was impossible for a demon to bleed out or really die unless they were sucked dry by another supernatural.

Mason would probably raise his hand first, followed by the rest of the remaining council.

Each of them had their reasons for despising me. Even though I was on their side, they would always see me as a demon.

One with a blue soul pulsing inside his body right alongside a very dangerous used one who never seemed to let me forget it.

I shoved the thought away and jerked as Mason pulled skin from my hand and then held it up front of his face. "You did it?"

"I'm a werewolf. I can do anything," he said smugly.

Searing pain stabbed my skin, running up and down my arm like tiny needles pressing into my flesh over and over again.

When I looked down…

The skin was back right along with the tattoo.

We both stared.

"Huh." Mason stood. "Well we tried."

"That's it?" I roared. "We *tried*?"

"You could always ask Ethan to bite it off." he grinned.

"Yes. A vampire biting my palm sounds lovely. Where do I sign up?" I jumped to my feet and ran my healed hand over my blond, almost white, hair. That was the other problem.

Changing.

I felt like I was changing.

For one, my ever-present horns had completely disappeared. I thought it was because my soul had been restored a year ago, because I had elf blood running through my veins compliments of a shady past and new friends I'd just made in the future, like Hope, the only remaining Elf princess, currently hitched to a male siren who I dreamed of killing on an hourly basis.

"Any luck?" A male voice that sounded like multiple orgasms and heat piped up, sweeping into the room.

I glared in Alex's direction. "Speak of the devil."

"I'm much better looking." He grinned, his jet black hair had shots of orange in it today; it changed depending on his mood.

"Feeling horny are you?" I pointed to the orange streaks in his hair.

And got flipped off.

"Hope's out with the girls... You know I don't do well when I go without skin-to-skin contact for too long."

"How sad for you..." I said, dripping with sarcasm, "You

do know that some people go hours, days, weeks, and yes, years without sexual contact?"

Alex just looked at me with horror lining every pretty feature, and on cue, the plant near the door started to lean toward him and then it wilted.

Nature couldn't help it.

I was more shocked that he'd mated in the first place.

I think everyone was.

A war was brewing. Then again, I'd been alive for thousands of years; a war was always brewing even in times of peace.

My head suddenly ached with thoughts I didn't want, with memories that tasted like blood, and with images of kills I couldn't forget.

I was born as the first of the demon race.

King.

Or so I'd thought—until the tattoo started itching, until I started seeing *him*, seeing them—so many Pharaohs, the sands of Egypt. See? Disconcerting.

Power surged beneath my skin, my fingertips buzzed with energy as I sidestepped Alex and made my way outside.

In a moment of complete insanity, I'd driven to Ethan's house, where most of the council lived since it was protected by both vampires and werewolves, and asked for help.

And gotten Mason of all people, gruff, pinecone-eating, long-haired, recently married, Mason.

I stared up at the stars and wondered how many more lifetimes I would get the chance to stare, when a ticking time bomb was pulsing on my hand.

"Deep in thought, are you?" Came Cassius' familiar voice.

His purple feathers wrapped themselves around his massive body as he walked toward me like he wasn't intimidating as hell.

Part archangel, part fallen, part, who the hell knew? He was the King of the immortals while Mason was King of the actual earth, the soil.

Alex, well he was the King of sex and himself and something else that none of us ever discussed because it was too painful to imagine how much power he had surging through his body.

Stephanie, mated to Cassius, was the last remaining true Dark One, a mixture of human and archangel with dangerous powers.

And a few weeks ago, we had discovered that Mason's mate was part goddess.

Basically it was as if the supernatural world had shit all over us in the span of a year just to see what we would do when they changed the game.

Another shiver ran over me.

The goddess.

She'd said she wanted to be entertained.

Well, what else could she possibly want? We were a complete shit show now!

"My tattoo seems permanent," I finally found myself saying as Cassius tucked his wings away until they disappeared into thin air like they were never there to begin with. "So that's a fun development."

"Fun." Cassius grinned. He rarely grinned. I narrowed my eyes just waiting for a feather to drop from his body and incinerate anything near my feet.

"Don't say fun, it sounds strange coming from someone who glares more than he smiles."

"You should talk," he fired back.

I sighed. "This again?"

"You've been different ever since Mason reclaimed his throne... you flew back to Seattle with your tail tucked between your legs—"

"Demons don't have tails."

"And you've been moping in that dark dungeon you call a house. Stephanie says she brings you food, you don't eat. Mason offered to hunt for pinecones, I told him no."

"Thanks for that."

"Small favors." Cassius folded his bulky arms across his chest. His pitch-black hair hung down his back, shining like the night sky. Blue eyes seemed to penetrate to my souls, both of them, the good and the bad. At least the good had tamped down the borrowed one. "It will be time to choose... soon, Timber."

"Choose?" My eyebrows arched. "I hope you're not under the assumption that because I've been helping the council that I need to mate like everyone else... I'm fine by myself. I like it that way."

Lies. Lies. Lies.

I was so damn good at lying I scared myself.

Centuries of practice.

Something I shouldn't be proud of but, meh, demon, cut me some slack.

"We all have journeys. Rarely are they easy," he said cryptically. "You've been running away from yours for a long time."

A vision of stumbling through the desert assaulted me before I shoved it away and snorted out a laugh. "This again? Look at me?" I spread my arms wide. "I'm the Demon King for shit's sake. I've been alive longer than half the people in that house. I've murdered, I've stolen. Don't for one second think that a little elf with the power to restore demonic souls saved me. I'm beyond saving." I didn't realize how much I meant it until I said it out loud.

A soul didn't forgive sins of the past.

It only saved you from a damned future.

I hung my head and then gave it a shake. "Never mind, I'm going to go home."

"Alone?"

"Well I do have a roommate now thanks to you." I said in a dry tone. "Whoever thought sending me a werewolf was a good idea?" I held up a hand, forestalling his answer. "Doesn't matter, I'll discover and kill them later."

"Be gentle. He's young."

"He's seven hundred years old. He'll be okay." I rolled my eyes and stalked off. Gravel crunched beneath my boots as I made my way over to my black Ferrari. The engine came alive with a growl, and I gripped the steering wheel until my knuckles turned white.

Empty.

So empty.

I hated that feeling.

The hunger that accompanied it.

That was one thing you never learned as a demon, that no matter how many souls you've been fed…

You will always want.

That was the great cruel joke of being a fallen race.

You were still lacking in every way, still wanting more. I still craved the taste on my lips as I took a life and relished in their death. Hunger pains assaulted until I had to close my eyes to shut them out.

And when I opened them, all I saw was red until slowly, the blue replaced it.

Always fighting.

Always two sides.

Hah, King of the demons.

I wondered what they would all say if they knew the truth… That I wasn't just a demon… never have been, never would be.

CHAPTER TWO

TIMBER

I was maybe one mile into my drive when my cell went off.

"Give me good news, Saint." I grunted as one of my associates chuckled on the other end, ah, it wasn't going to be good. And the day was going so well wasn't it?

"Sorry, Timber, Tarek's working out just fine."

I almost exhaled in relief. It's not like a werewolf, especially a royal one, knew how to be polite around so many demons, it wasn't in their nature to befriend something dark, no it was in their nature to completely destroy it with their bare teeth, and yet I had him working at one of our bars. What the hell had I been thinking?

Oh, right…

Give him a chance.

Let him see something outside of his home in Scotland, allow him to get groomed for the role he would eventually take by Mason's side as his younger brother, blah, blah, blah, blah—oh, look a hummingbird, blah.

"So what's the problem?" I was already turning around and making my way into the city. I owned a dozen bars around the Puget Sound, my largest was called Soul, get it? Soul? Because none of us had one, and we used it as a way to lure humans into our sanctums and suck them dry.

But those were the good ol' days.

Now my race was divided between those who wanted redemption, who, when we did leave this earth, wanted to be reunited with the Creator… and those who looked forward to the Abyss, Hell, Tartarus—whatever you called it, it didn't have unicorns and sunshine.

There weren't many left that were fully dark, but the ones that were, seemed to keep to themselves. I'd cleaned every bar up and only allowed my men to feed on a woman if she was willing.

We had a hell of a Non-disclosure agreement.

Then again, they were so high on our blood that they just nodded and walked out the door where our vampire security made sure they never remembered a thing.

It was working.

So why was I getting a call?

"Listen, someone came in asking for a job…" Saint grunted.

"We have enough people," I barked in a loud voice as I took the exit, waited at the stoplight and then hit the accelerator toward the Pier.

"That's what I said, but Tarek felt bad, and he—"

"Is Tarek suddenly making himself the manager?"

"No, but he is quite… persuasive."

I just bet he was.

"I'm pulling up now."

Rage filled me, feeding the darkness within as I slammed the door and stomped past security into the dimly lit bar with its loud pumping music and sweaty bodies, people all touching one another on the dance floor. Standing room only, why was I not surprised?

Like I said, we were like a drug to humans; once they were in, they were known to dance until we kicked them out.

Something about us just called to them.

They thought it was the beauty on the outside.

Joke was on them, because it was the ugliness on the inside that called, the darkness that matched their own. People are under the assumption that they're only attracted to good.

Spoiler alert.

Humans are fallen.

Meaning they're equally attracted to pure evil.

I grinned at that, even though I knew I shouldn't. My blue eyes searched the grinding bodies and finally stopped when I saw Tarek wave a huge hand in my direction.

The guy was at least six foot three and had long brown hair he pulled into a man bun that made me roll my eyes every time I had to look at him. He was a Scottish hippy in an American bar.

I had to hand it to him.

The guy raked in the tips every time he opened his bloody mouth.

"Tarek." I dug my fingernails into the wooden bar and then scratched into it a very graphic design of me hanging him over a tree and using a baseball bat to show him why hiring without my decision was a poor choice in life.

He just grinned down at the little fingernail drawing and said, "That's cute."

"You're a pain in the ass." A growl thundered in my chest earning cautious looks from people nearby. I gave my head a shake as the red threatened to take over my line of vision. "You've been here a week and already you've fired two people and then hired a person… Who died and gave you my job, because I'm pretty sure my heart's still beating."

"Pretty sure or *sure*-sure?" His eyes narrowed.

I let out an annoyed sigh. "I'm alive, which is more than I can say about you if you don't explain yourself in the next three seconds."

He gave me a smug grin. "So there was this woman…"

"Well shit, by all means, give her the keys to the place!" I roared, just as a short pixie looking thing rounded the corner, she had blue streaks in her hair, a nose piercing, and was wearing a tiny tank top paired with cut off shorts and red cowboy boots.

"As I was saying…" Tarek elbowed me like we were friends and then winked. "There was this woman—"

"Shouldn't women be taller?" I wondered out loud.

"Does it matter? Look at her."

"She's passable," I lied.

"Bullshit. She's gorgeous, and she begged me for a job."

I jerked my gaze to his. "Was she willing to do anything, then? You're a dog, a complete mutt, I should put you down…"

"Slow your roll Demon King," He grinned again. "I've got a girl back home I've had my eye on for a few hundred years."

My right eye twitched. "Well, by all means, move slower."

He lifted two middle fingers. "She's special."

"Yes that's why you should wait five hundred years to hold her hand—she's special, different. Tarek, I was fighting wars before your people were even gifted with the rule over earth. Believe me when I say, all of them are the same."

"Hi!" A peppy voice had me craning my neck and then looking down… down… down. The woman was barely five feet tall! "I'm Kyra Apollonia!"

I stared and stared, then crossed my arms and muttered. "You've got to be shitting me."

My tattoo seemed to shiver across my palm, the pain dissipated briefly before coming back full force like it was warning me about something.

Fantastic.

"What the hell kind of name is Kyra Apollonia?" I just had to know. Really. Who has the last name Apollonia? It was like Pollyanna but worse.

"Oh," Her bronzed cheeks seemed to pinken a bit. "So my parents are from this super old Greek family. Long story short, my father was Egyptian, my mother was Greek, and they wanted to combine both traditions. So Kyra Apollonia it is!"

"Kyra." I repeated her first name. "Or Kyros, like Ra, the sun." The room tilted as she sucked in a breath and then her jaw went slack.

I turned my attention back to Tarek. "Is she good?"

The infuriating thing waved a hand between us. "Hello? Standing right here? And how'd you know that? Did you study Egyptian mythology or something?"

I barked out a laugh at that. "Your mythology is my Bible, strange, but true." I rolled my eyes and looked back to Tarek. "If she breaks one glass she's done."

Silence ensued between them.

I sighed. "Multiple glasses then…"

"Thank you!" The woman I hardly knew, who barely came up to my chest, wrapped her arms around my body so tight and fast that I couldn't prepare myself.

I stood there like an idiot while her warmth filled me from the inside out. Every part of her body that touched mine was on fire, the good kind, the slow burn that makes you willing to do anything, say anything, swear anything for more.

And then she was gone, skipping back through the crowd and finding her place behind the bar pouring beer.

"Still think she's just like every other woman?" Tarek put a hand on my shoulder.

I was irritated that he put a hand where she'd touched.

He stole her warmth, damn it!

My eyes narrowed. "She's… there's something…" I squeezed my hands and then looked down at my palm.

The black seed tattoo.

Had sprouted a green branch.
Toward my thumb.

CHAPTER THREE

KYRA

If he didn't want me breaking glasses he needed to leave. I tried not to stare, but he was making it difficult. For one thing, he was completely massive. Then again, so was Tarek.

I frowned.

"What's his name?" I asked once Tarek came back behind the bar with an easy grin on his face and a wink in my direction. Surrounded by beautiful men, what a hardship.

"Who?" Tarek popped the caps off two Bud Lights and set napkins down for the customers in front of us, the ones who kept staring at me like I was on the menu. Bastards. I glared, then Tarek's eyes did this creepy thing that almost made me want to look away before both guys got up and left.

"What did you just do?"

"Nothing," he said quickly. "What were we talking about?"

"The guy that was ready to fire me for breaking glasses."

And as if I'd conjured him, he walked near the bar and held up two fingers. Tarek nodded and sent two bottles of jack sailing down the table. The guy picked them both up and walked off.

"The owner," Tarek said. "His name's Timber, he has a shit ton of money and needs a friend."

Goosebumps erupted across my skin at the word friend. I didn't have friends, and what family I did have just moved overseas. In fact, the last thing my mom said to me was that she had a good feeling about this bar. What mom says that? Specifically, about a bar named Soul? I took a deep breath and asked. "Say what?"

Tarek pointed at himself, "I'm the friend. He just doesn't know it yet. He likes to isolate himself, darkness and all that." He shot me a wink.

"So you just offered yourself up as his friend and he said 'sure thing, I'd like one of those!'" I laughed.

"Not exactly." Tarek joined in with me. "But it's important. He's going to need people around him."

"Going to?"

Tarek swallowed and then shrugged. "Let's just say I know things."

"Ohhhhhh," I tapped my temple with a black fingernail.

"So you're like one of those clairvoyant people?" That at least explained the goosebumps and weird feeling I'd had ever since walking in that place. A bar shouldn't feel warm and homey—and yet the minute I stepped over the threshold it did.

He flashed me a perfect white smile and leaned in until our mouths almost touched. "Why? Is that the sort of thing that does it for you?"

I shoved him playfully away, the last thing I needed was to get involved with a guy who reminded me of my parents. They thought they were clairvoyant too. "Didn't you say you had a girlfriend?"

"Yup! I'm safe." Another flashy grin before he sauntered off toward a table full of college students that looked ready to flash him if he so much as flinched.

I gave my head a shake and wiped off the bar with a wet rag when I smelled it. It was a pine scent that reminded me of frankincense mixed with something heady. My tongue felt thick in my mouth.

"Are you going to rub a hole into my bar too?" came the raspy voice.

Slowly, I turned.

Up, up, up I looked into ocean blue eyes and blond, almost white hair. A jaw so sharp I almost reached up to touch it, full lips that couldn't be real, and a body that seemed like it had stepped right off the cover of some magazine.

"Timber." I said his name out loud, testing it on my tongue. Great, more goosebumps erupted as the heat in my chest seemed to expand out toward my arms until my fingertips tingled.

He went completely rigid, his jaw clenched. "Well? You must need something if you're saying my name." He stepped forward, nearly pinning me against the bar. "So? What is it? Kyra?"

I blinked.

Was it my imagination or did he say my name with an accent?

His black pupils bled into the blue of his iris's and then I saw a pinpoint of red before he closed his eyes, turned around, and left, slamming the door to the bar behind him.

"What was that about?" Tarek asked making me jump a foot before pressing a hand to my chest. "He looked ready to either kill you or eat you."

"Hah." My heart fluttered, and then my entire body went on high alert. He was dangerous.

Very, very, dangerous.

And as I looked around the bar at the grinding bodies, at the beautiful people who watched others dance only to beckon them to their laps and toy with them like they were trying to put them under a spell, I had to wonder... why?

Just why?

Something felt... off.

Why had my mom suggested this bar of all places as a break after college?

"Tarek..." I licked my lips. "Why aren't any of the men dancing?"

He shrugged. "Probably because it's more fun watching women move their hips. Besides, not many men can dance, and men usually want sex so... clapping and snapping between beats typically means a hard no by any girl watching."

"You clap when you dance?" I laughed behind my hand.

He bowed. "And my point is made!"

I forgot about Timber the rest of the night.

And when I let myself in my small apartment down the street. The one I could barely afford.

I could have sworn I saw his face when I closed my eyes.

What was more disconcerting…

It felt like he was still watching me.

Even then.

Something was hot against my face.

The darkness wrapped itself around me like a blanket. Thankfully, it didn't scare me, the darkness. It was just the opposite of light, and that didn't mean it was bad.

Dark was just the absence of light.

I'd always preferred it. Always. As if it was my savior. Most little girls are afraid of the dark—I embraced it because it provided comfort.

But the light always came.

Sadly, in the morning, things would look the same.

I'd be the same.

I was safe in the shadows and in the light.

I closed my eyes as a heaviness settled on my chest.

And when I blinked them open, there he was, standing there.

I blinked again.

Gone.

I jolted up. "Timber?"

Nothing.

With a shiver, I lay back down and could have sworn I

heard someone chuckle in the darkness like this was the best entertainment they'd ever had.

And I was exhibit A.

CHAPTER FOUR

TIMBER

"It grew?" Ethan gave me an odd look, his green eyes flashing as his fangs descended like they were in danger and he needed to attack anyone and everyone. Then again, I was the one who was at the vampire's house with his wife Genesis and kids. "What do you mean it grew?"

But Ethan was the historian of the group. Next to Cassius, he was the only one who would know something, he wasn't as old as me, but it was close, plus who truly kept track when you'd been alive so long?

I let out a long sigh then showed Ethan my palm. A black seed tattoo was still in the middle like always, moving, pulsing like it was a living breathing thing. And then the small green branch had strained toward my thumb and was now wrapped like a ring around the base.

The door slammed open, Mason stomped in looking every inch the weird werewolf Watcher that he was.

A werewolf king with the blood of the Watchers running through his veins making him powerful as hell, who could keep track of all the supernatural shit going on in that place?

Dark hair hung past Mason's bare shoulders as he walked barefoot into the house, his wife Serenity, a relative goddess, close by.

I tensed.

Anything to do with goddesses made me want to run in the opposite direction. Mainly because it was my one weakness.

Or had been.

Her.

A daughter of Danu.

Twice a year she was allowed into this realm, twice a year I would touch her, and now... now the twelve goddesses of old were here permanently.

Because times were a changing.

Lovely.

Humans were no longer safe from the supernatural. And I had a sick feeling that it was only a matter of time before myth became reality.

"Serenity." I bowed my head in respect, but didn't stand. It pissed her off, which I loved more than she would ever know. She still had human blood in her body, but she was wholly goddess, wasn't she? You could tell by the softness of her skin, the way she smiled, the sizzle of power that erupted from that same smile.

She skipped over to me and pulled me in for a hug. "I missed you."

Mason growled.

"Sheath your claws." I rolled my eyes, returning her hug. "I missed you too, I've been busy at the bar and with... whatever the hell this is..."

She released me and looked down at my palm. "Wait, did you add to the tattoo?"

"If I wanted to add to any of the tattoos on my body do you think I would go for a tree branch? I mean honestly..."

She gave me a shove and then reached out and pressed a finger to the middle of my palm, pressing the seed as if it were a button.

A groan escaped my lips as the pulsing and itching got worse. The color faded from the green only to return brighter.

"I tried." She gave me a forlorn look. "I mean if none of us can remove it, your only hope is Cassius, but it's kind of cute, you know? It builds character for the big bad Demon King to have a fruit plant on his palm."

I wiped my hands down my face. "Call it a fruit plant again..."

"FRUIT PLANT!" Alex came barreling into the room and then spread his arms wide. "I've been waiting for this day my whole existence, the day you go soft."

"Does he have to be here? Right now?" I asked Ethan.

"He lives here." Ethan sounded as horrified as I felt, that

a male siren would be anywhere near any living breathing thing.

"Uncle Alex, Uncle Alex!" Ethan's twins stumbled into the kitchen, for being half vampire they were growing at alarming speed, already walking and talking like three-year-old's at only a year. Frightening to say the least. "Come jumpy with us!"

"Yes, go jumpy Alex. Maybe you'll jumpy so high up in the sky you stay there." I said dryly.

He laughed and chased the kids out followed by his very pregnant wife who glared in my direction. "If he flies high in the sky you better be ready to play dad," Her eyes narrowed in on mine. For an elf she was quite violent when pregnant.

And aggressive.

"I love you too." I winked at Hope as she made her way outside yelling at Alex to stop aggravating the trees under the trampoline. The earth shook a bit, pebbles grumbled.

All in all, a typical day in the life of a siren.

"So?" I squeezed my hand while Ethan pulled out another dusty book and dropped it on the kitchen table. "Am I going to turn into a plant? I don't think I could survive if I grew fruit." I tried to joke, but inside, I was petrified.

Which was alarming since I'd never once in my existence ever been afraid.

But now? I was drowning in fear.

Fear that the monster inside was finally coming out to play.

Fear that the borrowed soul was going bad.

Fear that my actual soul, the one that had been restored to me, was somehow dying, or fighting a losing battle against all the rest of the darkness within me that was overpowering every good decision, every good part of me.

I could feel the darkness closing in, and I didn't know how to stop it. All my life I'd wanted to one thing.

To be redeemed.

What cruel twist of fate would make it so I could taste that sort of existence only to have it ripped away from me?

Mason grabbed another book.

Serenity did the same.

Silence ensued as each of us read dusty book after dusty book, looking for clues in the only way we knew how.

Our old texts.

Each book told a story of our races.

Like I said, everyone had a Bible, this was ours.

Ethan shook his head. "Nothing recorded for the vampires."

Mason made a choking sound. Just as the door swung open revealing Tarek. "Sorry for barging in."

The guy pulled out a chair and put his feet up on the table.

Mason shoved them off.

Tarek put them right back on.

Brotherhood seemed fun.

"Something you need?" Mason asked

"Nope, was just too depressed to go back to the dungeon aka the demon's house." He grinned at me then said, "Just in case you weren't aware that's where you live."

"Thanks," I bit out. "Because I often get confused about my own identity."

Something sizzled against my skin and then it felt like

claws were ripping me from the inside out. I shifted to keep from bringing attention to myself, to the pain, to what was happening inside my own body.

Tarek shrugged. "What are we doing?"

"Reading." I drew out the word. "If you want to help all you have to do is open one of these," I slid one of the texts toward his feet and pointed. "And sound out the really hard words."

He flipped me off.

I ignored it and grabbed another text from the pile.

Nothing about tattoos so far.

Nothing about goddesses cursing demons either.

I cringed just as the air around us started to pulsate. "I hate it when he does that."

Cassius just appeared in a flurry of purple feathers, jet black hair, and the smell of ambrosia.

With an irritated sigh, I waited for him to sheath his wings. He tucked them back and then they completely disappeared like they were a figment of our imaginations. But we all knew, they were there, each feather was soft with razor sharp edges just pulsing to draw blood.

"I doubt you'll find anything in these." He shoved one of the texts away and stared at me, then grabbed my hand. "Incredible."

"Thanks, I've always wanted to hold hands with an angel."

"Angels and demons," Ethan said under his breath.

It earned him another sigh.

Was that all I was capable of, then?

My mood darkened just as ice spread through my veins,

compliments of the guy still holding my hand like we were minutes away from an awkward prom photo.

"Strange." Cassius examined my hand closer. "The ice doesn't chill the tattoo, only the skin around it."

"So you're saying I'll have frostbite everywhere but where I want it?" I nodded. "Fantastic, I'd say it's been a great day, but…"

Cassius eyes flashed white. "We'll figure it out. The good news is we have time, remember? We're at a standstill with The Watchers, and everything seems to have gone back to normal."

The Watchers were all fallen angels. Wonderful folks with way too much magic and a huge chip on their shoulders. Mason had given them all they'd wanted: the ability to listen to the heavens and hear the music of creation on a daily basis with the promise that if they behaved they'd be reunited once and for all.

It was a wonderful fairy tale I still had trouble believing.

Because if the worst of the worst could be welcomed into heaven.

What exactly did that say about me? About my race?

The thought haunted me.

It made me question everything about myself, everything about the world I knew, and I hated not knowing answers.

"The Watchers," Mason said in a gruff voice. "One of them may know…"

Cassius gasped and then doubled over, the entire room dropped forty degrees. I sucked in a freezing breath as Cassius gripped me by the shoulders.

"The hell?" Ethan jumped to his feet while Cassius held

me in his grasp like he was minutes away from slitting my throat. "Cassius? What are you doing? It's Timber."

"The sun." Cassius's voice shook the house. "Who houses the sun?" And then his eyes turned black, hard as stone as he whispered. "Ra."

And just like that a memory washed over me, it was brief, it was warm, everything I touched turned to light, my armor was red and gold, I marched in front of an army all arrogance and smiles.

"For your arrogance, I curse you!" Ramesses yelled. I only laughed and shook my head, Pharaohs, idiots all of them! A human couldn't curse me!

"I would like to see you try!" I let out a deafening roar as my brothers and sisters raised their swords. "This earth is ours!"

So much blood.

So much death.

I lost the light.

I reached for it—but the minute I stepped away from His face, the gift was gone.

As was the warmth in my chest.

Only emptiness.

A punishment for our sins.

For following Those who Watched the humans from the mountain, for choosing humanity first, the Creator second. For daring to believe we should have more than the idiot humans ruining the very planet we'd been ruling for centuries!

I jerked away from Cassius—or at least tried to.

And when he didn't budge, I let out a roar and slammed my hand into his chest.

He went flying backward against the wall, knocking over a few chairs and creating a giant crack that went all the way to the ceiling.

"What the hell was that?" Ethan was at Cassius's side in a second.

Cassius's eyes returned to blue, and they didn't leave mine as he stood, dusted himself off, and asked what was currently pulsing in my heart, in my head. "What sort of being can shove an angel and live to tell about it?"

I swallowed the dryness in my throat and hung my head. "I wish I knew."

Mason looked at me through narrowed eyes.

Tarek seemed unfazed.

And the noise was enough for Alex to be stomping back into the house ready to kick ass with everyone else.

I had always been their enemy.

And then their friend.

Now I wasn't sure what they would call me.

Because I'd just been able to shove away our King.

And everyone knew, demons couldn't touch an angel in any sort of violent way without getting the shit beat out of them.

Demons seduced.

We drained.

We did not fight.

And if we did, we did it as an army so we knew we would win.

A demon and an angel.

It was laughable.

More confused than before, I quietly stood, grabbed my keys, and left the house.

Feeling darker than ever.

My palm pulsed.

My heart ached.

And for some irritating reason—I thought of her, the beautiful girl with name like sunshine.

And for the first time in millennia, I felt my face heat.

CHAPTER FIVE

KYRA

I had a double shift that day, apparently they weren't just short staffed, they needed to hire another person after me. Tarek said it was because people quit only a few weeks in because they couldn't handle the stress.

I wasn't sure what was so stressful about a bar full of drunk people. I mean the entire place was beautiful when it wasn't crowded at least. The lights were a silver blue pointed toward the dance floor, all of the tables and chairs were white, and they had a wooden bar that extended all the way across the room. It was classy, unique.

Just… crowded.

I checked my phone and frowned. My parents were on another dig, I swear all they did was search for mythological things that never existed in the first place. I'd been sad when they left the US again and even more confused when my mom looked at me as if I was the reason they were leaving. I shoved my phone back in my purse and shoved it in the employee locker then pulled my short hair back into a ponytail. After washing my hands I made my way toward the bar to set up the menus. Tarek was already pouring booze into bottles.

He pulled out two small shot glasses and dumped tequila in them. "Cheers! You're going to need it today."

I stared him down in confusion. "We can't drink on the job."

"Correction, we shouldn't drink on the job, and normally I'd agree with you, but trust me on this," He slid the shot glass over. "You'll wish you would have had at least ten of these. Trust." He grabbed a wash rag and started wiping up the bar just as the front door opened.

I wasn't aware slow-motion walking actually happened in real life.

In movies, sure, they slow it down, edit, boom, you have the perfect entrance. But it wasn't reality.

At least I didn't think it was.

But I was fully experiencing it as Timber walked into the bar, his white blond hair looking like a halo over his head. His eyes went from what I could have sworn was red to a bright blue, and the smirk on his face, well let's just say I averted my eyes because I was one hundred percent sure my heart couldn't handle it.

Who looked like that and owned bars? Wasn't he missing the Academy Awards or something?

I tried to busy myself despite the sudden heat I felt in my chest, and then realized I was literally staring at a shot glass, on the clock, and looking guilty.

"Day drinking?" He breezed past me.

"No."

"Good." He took my shot, downed it, and grumbled. "Wish it worked better."

"Want me to pour you another?"

The corners of his mouth tilted into what felt like a mocking smile. "You could give me several bottles and I promise I could still drive home. It doesn't work well for some people. I'm one of those people."

"That's physically impossible," I pointed out trying not to stare too hard into his eyes, eyes that looked familiar.

"And yet... here I am." He grabbed one of the bottles in front of me and then disappeared back into his office. Huh, so maybe that was why he owned bars. Alcoholic? Wanted an excuse to sit at his desk with a bottle of Jack?

I shoved the thought away, grabbed some of the bar menus, and put them on the table just as the music turned on.

Timber chose that moment—what, like five seconds later?—to walk out of his office, deposit an empty liquor bottle on the bar, and say, "Told you."

He walked in a straight-line back; he looked tense, like he was upset that liquor had once again failed him some way.

"Impossible," I muttered under my breath.

"That…" Tarek appeared out of nowhere. "…seems to be the case with all things Timber, but I promise, what you see, is truly what you get."

I frowned. "He must have a high alcohol tolerance."

Tarek snorted.

"What?"

He held up his hands. "Hey if you want to test that theory," he eyed all the liquor bottles.

"I'm game." I shrugged. Nothing else to do since we weren't opening for another twenty minutes, besides there was something about him, something menacing and comforting all at once. He reminded me of the darkness, of my dreams, and I liked that more than I cared to admit. Great, two days in and I was acting crazy. "He likes Jack?"

"He likes to forget, and he needs to remember." Tarek said cryptically. "Then again what do I know, I'm just a bartender with a man bun."

"And a Scottish burr."

"And here I thought I hid it so well." He winked. "Not everything is as it seems, Kyra, remember that. Make the boss a drink, then get your ass back here to work."

"On it." I exhaled a breath and started mixing a concoction I'd seen on Facebook it was basically liquor on top of liquor on top of more liquor and finished off with beer. If that didn't do the trick—he wasn't human.

I snorted out a laugh at myself.

Right. What else could he be? A vampire.

I laughed again at myself, picked up the drink, and made the short trek to his office. The door was open. His eyes were locked on the screen of his laptop. "Did you need something person with the crazy name that makes no sense?"

"Oh good to know that's how you'll address me from here on out, kind of a mouthful don't you think?"

And nothing, no twitching lips, no smile, just... silence. And sighing.

The guy sighed a lot, like the world was a burden, like the air around him offended his person.

I'd met him, what? Twice? And I could already see that he just... wasn't happy, no containment, no inspiration, just this waste of male beauty and darkness.

Something warmed in my chest.

He just... he needed something to be excited about.

Right?

"Here," I walked fully into his office and set the drink down on the mahogany table. "You said booze doesn't work on you and well, I like a good challenge."

He eyed the drink skeptically. "Do you now?"

"Absolutely, if that doesn't knock you on your ass, I'll owe you."

"What?"

"Huh?"

"What will you owe me?"

"Umm," The air thickened around us. "What do you want?"

Electricity crackled between us, the air was heavy with... something. His eyes didn't leave mine. "I'll let you know once I win."

"Too bad you'll be completely drunk."

"We'll see." He grinned finally, took a sip, then another. "It tastes like you played suicide with liquor instead of soda."

"Best game ever, I always mixed my Mountain Dew with Doctor Pepper." I said trying to lighten the mood and the tension swirling in his eyes. He gave off heat and something else, cinder maybe? But that would be crazy.

"What a monster you must have been" He finally grinned. "And you haven't lived unless you've mixed coke with lemonade."

I made a face.

"Trust me," He winked and stood, then literally downed the rest of the drink in seconds before handing the glass back to me. "It was a valiant effort."

"Well, wait for it to kick in."

"I have a very aggressive metabolism." He shrugged.

I waited for him to laugh, slur, say he was tired, thank me, kiss me, I mean really any sort of behavior other than him just staring at me with big bright blue eyes and darkness in his pupils would have been better.

"About that favor…" He leaned in, his hand grazed mine as he pressed the glass farther against me. And then his eyes flashed red so brief I probably imagined a trick of the lights. His knuckles grazed mine and then he gripped my hand. The glass dropped onto his desk shattering into several pieces. He shook his head then leaned forward. "Did you drug me?"

"With liquor? Yes." I squinted, he seemed… brighter. "Are you okay?"

"You—" He leaned, swayed, then tightened his hold. "So many colors, like a painting, not dull at all. Like the desert, and heat, like the sun."

"Um… should I get Tarek?" I backed away even as my heart picked up speed at the way his eyes bore into mine.

"Don't you feel it? See it?" His eyes narrowed, and then he jerked his hand away from me and stared me down like I was a disease. "I should fire you."

"For giving you a drink?"

He exhaled a curse and rounded the corner of the desk. "Do not touch me again, ever. I don't know who sent you but no, the answer is no."

"No?" I repeated. "Timber I think you just had too much to drink—"

He burst out laughing. "It's not the alcohol. It's you."

"I make you drunk."

"I was going to say violent," he spat. "Stay away from me. This isn't a game. You'll only get hurt. Run along now." He flicked his wrist.

"Okay, I think I'll just grab some water for you and—"

In a flash he was bracing my body against the wall, holding me up like I weighed nothing, his teeth flashed, were those fangs? I blinked and then he looked normal again, his eyes blazed so blue they almost turned white and then he slowly lowered me to my feet. "Do. Not. Touch. Me."

"Okay."

"Don't speak to me," he added. "Don't look at me. As far as I'm concerned, you do not exist. Are we clear?"

I nodded as tears filed my eyes. And then I stumbled back to the bar, my heart feeling bruised, my ego more so. What did I do wrong? And why did a stranger's rejection make my heart clench?

"Bet you wish you would have taken that shot." Tarek

said with a smirk. "And don't worry, he can't help but be an ass, I'm convinced that it's next to his name in the dictionary, you know, demon, evil, ass, ahhh Timber, there it is!"

I tried laughing past the knot in my throat, it was a pathetic attempt. "A little extreme to call him a demon but yeah… that was… weird."

"Strap in," Tarek said under his breath and then he was gone, leaving another shot poured ready for me.

I took it.

Coughed.

And wondered if I should bring Timber something to sober up, only to see him breeze passed me like he hadn't just downed over two gallons of alcohol. "Tarek make sure she doesn't burn the place down."

I suppressed a growl.

Timber stopped at the door and very slowly looked over his shoulder and barked. "Wear more clothes tomorrow."

I looked down at my jean shorts and crop top. "I thought—"

"Don't think, do," he snapped slamming the door behind him.

Tarek held the empty shot glass in front of my face. "One more before your double shift."

"Like it will help."

"Let's just say I'll make sure it does…" he said cryptically and oddly enough, I trusted he would.

And even weirder?

I made the most tips I'd ever made at any bartending job.

And I actually felt good for the next eight hours.

I forgot all about my parents moving to another country.

I forgot about the disappointment they tried to hide whenever they asked if I'd found a job I liked or a guy that didn't completely turn me off. The answer was always no, I was always anxious, always moving, always searching.

Until now.

Until that night, even after the rejection, something about Soul felt right.

Like the world was a happier place than I originally thought.

Like I had a place in it.

CHAPTER SIX

TIMBER

It was two seconds.

Her touch.

Long enough for the room to spin, for my world to tilt as a mirage of rainbow-like colors erupted in my line of vision, they surrounded her like an aura, one that pulsed in perfect cadence to the tattoo on my hand.

Disconcerting, that's what it was.

Kyra was hiding something, or worse, it had been hidden from her, meaning she was a pawn in a very dangerous game that I wanted no part of. I thought that the games were over now that the werewolves were in their rightful place, now that the Watchers were done fighting us.

The main war was over.

And things were worse than before, because now the line between humans and the other worldly was slowly starting to blur into something else completely.

I'd never reacted to anyone's touch that way before—not Genesis, Serenity, or even Hope—a freaking elf and a friend.

I hit the accelerator so hard, it tapped the car floor, and my Ferrari sped toward the forest.

It was a last-ditch effort to get answers, the only way I knew how, to ask the oldest of the bunch what the ever-loving hell was going on.

I didn't want to face her again.

I didn't want to look at her and remember the nights spent in her arms, the stolen kisses, or the way she'd made me feel like a god.

It was forbidden.

No matter how much I craved it, and seeing her just made the hunger that much worse because I knew only she could quench my thirst, my need to be filled.

If I had any chance of surviving another century, I would ignore the pull toward her.

I hit the brakes and skidded to a stop, sending a cloud of dirt flying up around my car. When I killed the engine, silence roared in my ears. I walked away. No need to lock my doors; it wasn't like Bambi was going to steal my car—and if any human tried they'd be sent to the hospital in a nice body bag, and if they were lucky straight to the morgue.

I knew she would be here, Eris, the thorn in my side, the balm to my soul. The one woman I wasn't supposed to touch. In a cruel twist of fate, she was damned to serve the virgin goddess Danu and wasn't allowed to physically or emotionally attach herself to immortals or humans—especially the Demon King with creepy tattoos, but that wasn't the point.

She would at least have information I needed. She was old as hell, just like yours truly, and she knew the ins and outs of magic that seemed to create a pulse-like heartbeat in our world. Right on cue, my tattoo started to heat on my palm. It was getting bigger, something was growing inside me, I could feel it, could feel the need to break free—and I was afraid I knew exactly what was trying to break loose.

A soul trapped too long in a body not meant for it.

It felt like fingernails were digging against my insides, clawing away at my ribs—free—did I even know what that meant?

The gravel crunched beneath my boots as I made my way into the forest. I knew what I would find, visions of women bathing would be the only thing I saw for the next mile as I passed by the large river and entered into the land of the fae.

Danu and the other goddesses stayed on earth—that didn't mean they stayed in our realm.

Damn, it was going to be a rough night.

I gritted my teeth and passed two golden nymphs who waved in my direction and blew a kiss; both of them had white hair and razor-sharp teeth behind those plump lips. Petals flew in my direction, and I ducked, careful not to let them touch me; the last thing I wanted was to be imprisoned under a tree for the next decade just because I wanted to touch their petals.

And I mean *all* of their petals.

It was irritating to an immortal and quite damning to a human.

I passed under the cover of two large trees, their leaves changing from green to black as I made my way farther into the darkness of the forest.

I was used to the way things died around me, or should I say I had been used to it until recently—I'd forgotten how it felt to carry death with me, to know that I would always carry it—a curse of my species.

A curse of what I was.

Power pulsed through my fingertips as I knew it would any time I entered into the immortal realm.

Like my spirit was trying to remind me of my past.

A past I couldn't remember.

Fragments existed.

There was always so much burning, so much thirst, and the despair of loneliness couldn't be matched.

And then I gave it up, for what?

Something that was slowly trying to destroy me from the inside out.

I finally made my way to the meadow. Yellow daisies sprouted out from the tall green grass… And there Eris was, dancing in the field like I knew she would be. Her white dress was plastered against her body, her face lifted up toward the violet-tinted sky.

I squeezed my eyes shut as I took a step toward her, the flowers instantly died beneath my feet, I crushed their petals, bringing death and destruction through the meadow until I was finally right in front of her.

Yellow irises rimmed in blue locked onto me. "I knew you'd come."

"I always do." My voice echoed, another reminder.

I shook my head as pain splintered my temples.

"It's dying." She reached out and pressed a hand to my chest. "You know this, don't you?"

"What's dying?" I trembled at her touch.

Her cherry red lips pressed together in a firm line as her jet black hair whipped around her face, and then the wind just stopped, leaving us there while my darkness overtook the small space where we stood.

Flowers turned to ash.

The sky's hue darkened to a deep plum purple.

A chill filled the already icy air.

"You know what." Her eyes went wide. And then she jerked her hand away. It was coated in black soot, she pressed her fingertips together as ash fell to the dead ground beneath her feet. "You should go."

"No." I reached for her, and for the first time in my existence, the goddess who had taunted me, teased me, told me I was hers, turned her back on me.

I grit my teeth. "Nobody turns away from me!" My voice shook the realm, birds flew from the trees making their escape.

What the hell was happening to me?

"Once it dies, you'll remember everything, once it dies you won't want me anymore…" She shot me a cruel smile over her shoulder. "It's been fun, though, hasn't it?"

"Dies?" I replied, dumbstruck.

She lifted a shoulder, not answering, not really giving me

what I needed at all.

I showed her my hand, the seed that had now taken root, growing into a damn tree. "What is this?"

"Your curse," she whispered. "And your only chance at breaking free... Let it consume you and you may get everything you've ever hoped for. Ignore your true nature, turn away from your heart, from the restored soul you've been given, and you'll die."

"Demons don't die."

"No." Her smile was cruel. "But that's not what you are now, is it?"

"Bullshit." I was so tired of riddles, tired of games, just plain tired of everything. I grabbed her by the arm and jerked her against me. "You do not turn your back on the Demon King."

"I don't turn my back on him at all—few would live to tell about it—but you are not he." She jerked away. "The minute Hope restored you, she restored *all* of you. Your body is rejecting the used soul. It won't get better, not unless you choose."

"Choose what?" I was afraid to ask as shame washed over me. I was bad, death itself, wasn't I?

"True nature can never be denied, not even for someone as powerful as you." She took a step back. "You have been thirsty for so long, haven't you?"

Eris wiped the ash from where I'd touched as if she was cleansing herself from every thought of me.

"For years we've been as close as lovers," I reminded her. "And this is it?"

"You cannot touch me without killing me, Timber.

Before…" She sighed as a single tear ran down her cheek. "Before you could, but it's too late. Too late for us, we were doomed from the start, you know the rules. A goddess of the earth and a demon? It was bad enough, wasn't it? And now that you are… returning to your original state, there is no hope, not even if you devoured a hundred used souls. You are damned, prince of darkness." And then she bowed and disappeared from the valley.

I wasn't sure how long I stood there, long enough that the purple sky went to black, long enough that when I turned around and started walking back toward my car, the path was lined with crows, an honorless guard garbed in cloaks of black feathers.

Each of them with their eyes missing as if someone had purposefully poked them out so they would be blind to the world around them, to the darkness I carried with me.

Creepier than that.

When I finally left the realm of the fae and made it to my car, the darkness had followed.

I stopped walking and turned around as stark blackness filled my line of vision. It should have been impossible.

And yet there I was, surrounded by the very thing most people feared.

I had brought death to the human realm.

And I had no way of fixing it.

Other than calling on the immortal council and once again asking for help I wasn't sure they could even give.

With a cry, I slammed my hands onto the hood of my Ferrari and looked down as ash fell from my fingertips.

I was well and truly screwed.

CHAPTER SEVEN

KYRA

I hated how much I thought of him.

Timber left like the hounds of hell were chasing him. From next to me, Tarek snorted out a laugh like something I said was funny.

Only I wasn't talking.

"You okay?" I tossed one of the bar rags in his direction. He swiped it out of the air with his right hand and gave me an amused grin.

He was beautiful in a hipster sort of way.

Why wasn't I thinking of my new co-worker instead of my boss?

"Life and death are a lot like love and hate," Tarek said cryptically again like he could read my thoughts. His brown eyes went almost black as they darted back and forth as though reading an invisible book in front of his face. "One cannot exist without the other, counterparts exist to bring balance to the world, just like good and evil."

"O...kaayyyy..." I narrowed my eyes and was tempted to press my hand against his forehead to see if it was burning up. "Too many shots?"

He snorted out a laugh. "Not near enough, I have a fast metabolism." He patted his flat muscular stomach. No crap it was a fast metabolism, I saw him maul two burgers an hour ago, if I did that they'd have to roll me out of here.

I gave my head a shake. "Do you need help with anything else?"

"Nope." He shrugged and gave me the goofy grin I was used to. "You can go home. I'll make sure all the drunk college kids make good choices."

"Hah." I rolled my eyes. "They come in here to make bad choices not good choices."

"True." He winked and again I felt nothing, huh. "Go, just..." He sniffed, then sniffed again.

"Hey, are you getting sick?" I reached out toward him but he was already backing away and looking out the front window down the street. "Tarek?"

"Shadows," he whispered under his breath. "On second thought..." He shrugged. "I think I'll just walk you home."

"I live only a few blocks away," I pointed out. "And I have pepper spray."

He winced. "Yeah, pepper spray hardly keeps someone away if they're hell bent on killing you."

"Wow, great bedtime story, thanks!" I snatched up my purse and jerked my head toward the door. "You can follow me if you must…"

"I would be the most obedient dog, you have no idea," he teased.

And for some reason I had this vision of him with fur covering his body, golden eyes alert and watchful.

What the hell was wrong with me?

Our eyes locked. "After you," He put his hand on my back while I gave my head another good shake. The vision had been so clear.

"Right." I gulped and walked out of the bar and into the cool Seattle air. The streets were still filled with college students and the few random families out for dinner. It wasn't like we were in a crappy area of Seattle, so I wasn't sure why he felt the need to walk me, but I wasn't going to say no to company, especially after his weird warning.

He kept his hand on my back as we weaved through the crowds and even weirder it was like he was able to dodge people before he even knew which direction they were coming at us from.

I stared straight ahead and almost stumbled when I noticed a flicker in front of me, something dark, maybe a dog, moved to the right of my vision.

"Shit," Tarek grumbled under his breath and then fully wrapped an arm around me before jerking us off the sidewalk and into an alleyway where he pressed his mouth against mine before I could protest, his hands running up and down my arms like he was suddenly on fire for me.

I shoved against his chest only to have him move his lips down my neck, his teeth nipping my ear. "Go with it."

Maybe it was the tone of his voice, or the chill that suddenly wracked my body, but I nodded briefly before wrapping my arms around him.

It was a nice kiss.

Hot.

Aggressive.

But it felt like I was kissing my friend, my very good friend, and I was too confused to ask him why he suddenly felt the need to do that.

His kiss deepened, and then he pulled back, his eyes completely black. He gave his head a rough shake before dropping to his knees in front of me.

"Tarek!" I was starting to panic. He was a good guy, right? Right? He wasn't trying to take advantage of me? Was he? I was about ready to scream when his gaze softened.

"You smell like him," He said it so matter-of-factly that I had nothing, absolutely nothing to say back as Tarek straight up ran his tongue from the bottom of my calf all the way up to my bare thigh.

Chills erupted all over my body as the scent of cedar and pine mixed with the warmth of pumpkin and cinnamon, all my favorite fall scents filled the air. My knees almost buckled as I gripped his head, tugging his hair with my right hand, hauling him back toward my other leg.

A guttural moan erupted from the back of his throat as he

gripped my left leg with both hands and mauled me with his mouth like my leg was an ice cream cone and he wanted one more lick, or—God help me—seven. That *was* lick number seven, not that I was counting.

He gripped me by the ass, his fingers digging into my skin as he slowly looked up at me like he was ready for the main course.

And the main course was me.

Heat enveloped my core in pulsing waves as his scent filled the air around us, and then he jerked his head to the street sniffed and relaxed.

Panting, I was stunned as my arousal started to wear off like he'd just doused me in the strongest pheromone known to mankind.

I shook my head out of the daze. What was happening?

His eyes flashed back to brown, a trick of the moon maybe, as he stood to his full height, towering over me. Bracing me against the wall, he leaned in, his nose nuzzling my neck like he was a cat needing a bit of attention. "It's really too bad."

"What is?" I almost reached for him again as waves of heat pulsed off of him. "The fact that you tricked me and just wanted to make out or that you stopped?"

He stilled, pulled back just enough so I could see his brown eyes, at this angle they almost seemed to glow. "I was going to say it's too bad you've already been marked."

"Marked?" I repeated. "Like with a marker?"

His lips pressed together in a smirk. "Sure, let's go with that."

"Tarek." The voice was chilling and familiar, I quickly

jerked my head toward the street where Timber stood. "You can go now."

"You sure about that, boss?" Timber ground his teeth. "Because the way I see it—"

Timber held up his hand silencing Tarek faster than a trained puppy. "She's safer with me than with you, especially after that spectacular attempt at claiming what isn't yours."

Tarek jerked away from me, looking massive in the moonlight as he stared Timber down. "You know why."

"I also know when someone's tempted." His smirk was gorgeous, dangerous, as his eyes flashed. What was with the moonlight tonight? "Remember your place."

Tarek snorted out a laugh. "Funny, I was just going to tell you the same thing..." He purposefully bumped into Timber's shoulder and then whispered something I couldn't hear, but it was enough for Timber to look disappointed. Was I getting fired?

He nodded once to Tarek, put his hand on his shoulder, and then Tarek was gone and I was standing in an alleyway with the boss who threatened me and made me cry.

Fantastic.

I think I would choose whatever chilling thing was out in that street than the boss whose eyes seemed to look right into my soul like he wanted to either devour it or just claim it as his own.

I wrapped my arms around my body and stared him down. "I'll just be going..."

"And I'll just be following," he said in a voice I knew I couldn't argue with.

And because I was too tired to fight and just wanted to

get home without getting mauled or confused, I sighed and said, "Suit yourself."

We walked in silence for the next few blocks.

It wasn't until we were four blocks down that I realized every single person was walking on the opposite side of the street, which wouldn't be strange except it looked like they were purposefully crossing.

I frowned. "Did that person just bow?"

"He's probably high as a kite." Timber said with nonchalance, but I didn't miss the consistent eye contact he had with people like he was somehow bending them to his will.

Creepy.

It had just been a really long confusing day.

Sleep always made me feel better, and I always loved the dark anyway, I preferred the warmth of the hidden shadows, like the way Tarek had felt when he licked—

"Sorry." Timber bumped into me then gripped me by the arms. "I wasn't paying attention. I didn't mean to run over you."

We were at my apartment building already. It wasn't very new, but it did the trick and I had a load of locks and a ring camera, so I felt safe-ish.

"I don't like your apartment building." He eyed it up and down. "Too many windows."

"Some of us like a little light," I fired back. "Some of us aren't vampires."

I kept it to myself that I preferred shadows and a heavy darkness like a gravity blanket draping over me.

Timber gave me an amused look, his eyes lighting more

than I'd ever seen them like he was trying to hold in laughter and then he shrugged. "You're right, I'm much better looking."

I rolled my eyes. "And maybe if they existed I'd agree with you but… sorry fresh out of those so I'm just going to be heading inside. Thanks for walking me home."

"One minute." Timber reached out, his skin felt colder than Tarek's but still soft, so velvety soft that I let out a shocked hiss of breath when he somehow managed to pull me against his rock-hard body.

The problem? I let him.

And I had no idea why I was even letting him near me after today—after the kiss with Tarek, after the rejection from Timber himself. I hated girls like that, girls that wanted the guy they believed they could fix, the angry one with a chip on his shoulder, of course I'd be attracted to that guy not the one who said he'd be as loyal as a dog.

My body started to tremble like something was going to burst out of my soul.

"What?" I tried to act normal even as his eyes searched mine like he was reading my thoughts, trying to gauge my reaction to his touch and came up empty. "Is this your way of apologizing or just committing sexual harassment after hours? Newsflash even the boss can get in trouble for that sort of thing."

"And Tarek?" He didn't let me go. "A co-worker?"

I opened my mouth to explain but I realized I couldn't explain just like I couldn't explain why I was letting Timber touch me.

"Hmm, that's what I thought." He leaned in until our foreheads touched and then he just held us there.

I thought it was weird until I started to smell this intoxicating scent, like the most powerful flower in the world was permeating the air around us. "What is that?"

"Lotus—it cleanses."

"Cleanses what?" I shuddered.

"Ancient Egyptians used to use it during funeral rituals to cleanse the bodies before they descended into Hell."

"Or Heaven," I argued.

"That's almost adorable, that you still believe."

"You don't?"

He pulled back and gave me one of the saddest looks I'd ever seen in my entire life, his eyes empty, his face expressionless. "Heaven isn't for me."

"And it isn't for me?"

"I guess that all depends on you, now doesn't it?"

Enter the weirdest conversation I'd ever experienced.

Timber gave his head a shake. "Be safe tonight, keep your windows closed, you never know what some sort of depraved human might do when they see opportunity."

"Like you?" I crossed my arms.

He didn't even seem insulted; he just grinned. "Definitely not me, then again part of you knows that, the part that's locked up inside where I imagine butterflies and unicorns exist."

I rolled my eyes. "Yeah, okay, I'll see you tomorrow I guess."

And I could have sworn I heard the words. "And tonight in your dreams."

CHAPTER EIGHT

TIMBER

Egypt 336 BC

"Pharaoh." I eyed him up and down while he stared up at my golden throne. "Have you come to petition again?" I smiled darkly and popped a grape into my mouth. Its juices gave me life like all living things. "I guess it has been…" I looked up. "…ten days since your first request."

"Master." He fell to his knees in a swirl of smoke. His body was elsewhere, but his soul was kneeling before me, begging a favor… of me. I almost laughed, but it amused me more to see him on his knees. The fact that he, an evil man, would come and ask me for a favor in exchange for something so precious was wasted. Then again, I didn't have to tell him that, not when I enjoyed finally watching him show a sense of humility—I only hoped He was watching—maybe it meant there was hope, maybe not.

"Darius…" I yawned. "Tell me what it is you request, and we will see if the sacrifice is worth the outcome you desire."

"Power." He stood to his full height. "I want my descendants to know what I have done! I want a tomb in my name, with jewels for the afterlife, enough to secure me safe passage into the Creator's arms."

"Ah…" I tossed another grape into the air. "And this is where our beliefs differ, great king. You cannot live a life of depravity then buy your way into the Creator's arms. You say you want to be remembered yet I hear your people's screams in the darkest depths of this universe. You say you want jewels for the Creator when he has enough jewels to last him for several eternities. What you want is power over mankind, and that is something only given to the immortals. I cannot beseech your request when you do not ask the right favor."

"A riddle?" He snorted.

"A truth," I stated plainly, leaning forward, my long white hair fell to my belt in braids of black jewels. "You beg for life after life and you curse your people to their deaths beneath the rocks of their labor. Perhaps you'll grow a heart and come back and sacrifice the only thing worth having."

"Power?"

"Love." I sighed. "If you want all of these things, I will

grant you your favor, but your days will be numbered and the days of your family, your wife, your children. If you do not give your people the love they deserve, your contract will be canceled and your soul extinguished immediately while your enemies take over your kingdom—now do we have a bargain?"

I could see it in his eyes. He would sacrifice all and he would sacrifice nothing to do it.

He was damned already.

"Yes, immortal, take it all. I will change, they will love me."

I nodded and waved him away as the mist started to disappear, he turned his back just as I reached across the distance, pulled his soul from the darkness, and placed it in the iridescent bowl next to my throne. After all, favors are never truly free are they?

"No, Darius," I whispered. "You will not change, because you are a fool who thinks he can rule without his heart, and now that I hold your soul for promise of payment you will fail." I shook my head. Humans. Would they ever learn? I reached down and scratched the tattoo on my arm and frowned.

The itching intensified.

And then I shot out of bed in a cold sweat.

"Who the hell is Darius?" Mason was literally hovering over my sweat-soaked body with nothing but my favorite red grapes in his right hand and an upside-down book in the other.

"Could you not stand over me when I sleep?" I scowled. "How long have I been out? And why the hell are you here?"

A headache pierced my temples. I rarely slept, I was a demon, after all; what need did I have for sleep? But lately it had been getting worse and worse. Was the tattoo the cause? The effect?

And the dreams.

So vivid, lifelike, so very familiar and yet wrong at the same time.

"Darius." Mason repeated. "Who is he?"

Was he my old soul? Was that the borrowed soul I'd been given? Was he trying to tell me something? That he needed to return to the physical body long ago in the grave?

My head pounded worse.

"Me? Maybe. I don't know," I confessed, too tired to explain as I peeled off my clothes and stepped into the walk-in shower.

Mason just bit into his grapes. "You been working out?"

"Are all Watchers this annoying? Why couldn't you have just been full wolf? Still eating berries and pinecones?"

I could almost feel his shudder.

I quickly rinsed off and put a towel around my waist then stepped back out. "Also, could you stop eating all my food?"

"So, Tarek said he kissed a girl last night." Mason eyed me with amusement. "And then he said that he licked her... and then *boom*!" He clapped a hand against his denim-clad thigh. "You appear like a bad nightmare come to life."

"Boo." I pretended to be afraid then went to my huge walk-in closet. "Is there a reason you're here telling me this story? Or are you just out of people to annoy? Where the hell is Alex when I need him?"

"I have an answer for that, gardening." Mason cackled out a laugh.

"You're shitting me." I poked my head out of the closet. "Has he lost his mind?"

"No, get this, he thinks he can garden with nothing but his good looks, you know by forcing the tomato plants to grow. He and Ethan have a bet, then Cassius wanted in on it. And honestly I'm just enjoying not being at war right now, which I said to Cassius only to have him glare at me like I'd just challenged the universe in the wrong way. Then Tarek said something about the girl and a kiss and you, and I figured I'd come investigate."

"Lucky. Me." I growled, quickly finding clothes and tossing them on, then facing him again head on. "There's nothing to tell."

"Right, well the guys want to call a council meeting, seems that Cassius may have found something in one of the books about your little fruit tree tattoo."

I rolled my eyes. "For the last time, it's just… never mind." It was a damn fruit tree. And I officially hated everyone.

Mason grinned. "So tense these days. You know what fixes that? When you settle down and—"

"Demons don't mate."

"But you have a soul."

Two, actually. I just shrugged. "Doesn't matter, since it doesn't seem to be helping whatever this is," I waved my hand into the air and scowled.

"Just wait until we talk to Cassius. Want me to drive?"

At that I did laugh. "No. I'm never getting in a car with you ever again. I don't care that we don't die, it's petrifying."

He gave me a disappointed look, stupid dog. "I'm not that bad."

"You're right, you're worse." I felt him follow me into the living room as I grabbed my keys and then remembered that I needed to drive a different car because of… ahem, reasons.

"Where's the—"

"Don't ask." I said through clenched teeth. "I'll take the Tesla today."

"Hmmmm." Mason grinned. "Tarek said you had a busy day yesterday. Now I'm even more curious. Oh also…" He sniffed the air. "You smell like ash and sunshine."

I shook my head. "You need to work on your compliments, I always smell like ash. Demon, duh. And the sunshine is probably because it's coming out of your ass twenty-four seven hitting anything in its path."

"Aw," Mason touched his hand to his chest. "I knew one day we'd be best friends."

"Yes, here boy!" I slapped my thighs. "That's a good boy, sit boy, roll over."

Thunder literally erupted over the house as Mason's eyes went a creepy white.

"Stop with the tricks." I shoved him out of the way and went into the garage, and called over my shoulder. "Wanna race?"

I was out of the garage in seconds while he ran to his waiting motorcycle. And actually smiled as he tried to throw me from the road several times on our way to Ethan's.

He was right about one thing: at least I had a friend, even if I would die before admitting it to him.

An arctic coldness seeped through me when I realized that if I couldn't stop this, whatever it was, I would need to leave, because there was no way I would expose them—my friends, my family—to the darkness growing within.

By the time we made it to the house, Ethan was already waiting for us outside like he knew we would be there, stupid vampire. Cassius and Stephanie were casually flirting with one another which just made me wonder what sort of alternate reality was permeating the human race when angels and half angels were smiling like that at each other.

Disgusting.

Alarming.

Ignore the pain in my hand and on my chest.

Right.

And just like that, I saw the black inky dark mist in my car. I was bringing destruction to everyone, wasn't I?

I got out of my car and gave them a withering look. "Could you do that elsewhere?"

"No." Cassius just shrugged. Ah, so easy to work with. I just loved my co-workers. Ignoring him, I stomped into the mansion and went in search of something.

The information they had?

Silence?

Just something that would shake me out of my dream, out of the memories that kept attacking me from within.

The council all followed me back inside, Alex was in the library shocking the hell out of me by actually reading.

"What's that?" I snapped.

He yawned, didn't even look up. Oh goody, his hair was purple today—did that mean he was extra horny or just a little bit?

"Botany, you... dumb... ass." He said it slowly for my

benefit, fantastic. I let out a growl and nearly chucked a chair in his direction, but I restrained myself since I could sense his very intense need for a fight.

"Trouble in paradise?" I grinned menacingly.

"She's tired because I have strong sperm, and that's all you need to know." He finally looked up and winked. "So I need a hobby."

"And you chose botany?" I laughed.

"No." Alex stood and towered over his book. "I chose a challenge. You should see my garden compared to Mason's."

"Heard that." Mason was eating, *again*, as he walked into the library and then spread his arms wide, apple in his right hand, another cluster of grapes in his left, reminding me yet again of my dream. What the hell was going on? "Come on, Timber, I'll show you."

"Yes. Can't wait. I was hoping this would turn into garden hour…" I said under my breath as I followed them outside into the blinding Seattle light.

It never felt warm against my skin, the light, it just felt, invasive in a way that wasn't welcome; it made me want to crawl into a cave and sulk about all the ways the world had wronged me. Beyond that, light always reminded me of something I had lost which just made it even that much more painful to experience.

Strange, since Kyra smelled exactly like the sunshine surrounding me and that never bothered me the way the actual sun did.

Huh.

I let out a rough exhale and put on a pair of Ray Bans,

truly channeling my inner demon, and stepped out into the light.

I didn't realize the sort of mistake I had made until the smile fell from Alex's face, which was rare; he always found something to be amused about or with.

"Timber." Alex's voice boomed as I physically witnessed his power—he went from purple hair to fire orange with energy radiating around him. "What the hell are you doing?"

"Standing," I said through clenched teeth.

"Shit," Mason said under his breath, reaching out to me, "Just, step away from the garden."

I followed his gaze. My black shoes had barely touched the edge of the grass that led down to the garden, and already a small trickle of dead moved like a shadow toward the tomato plants slowly and surely causing the leaves to crinkle up and fall to ash.

"So," Cassius walked outside. "It's come to this?"

"Come to what?" Ethan looked down at my feet and then up into my eyes, and then he did the strangest thing, he put his arm out and blocked both fallen angels as if I was the bad guy when they could kick my ass—except for last time, I guess.

I frowned. I wasn't the enemy here, I was part of a fallen race, yes, but I had a restored soul now. I was good, I wouldn't kill them, at least not in their own home, and I sure as hell—

"...can he hear us?" Ethan asked right in front of me.

I opened my mouth to speak but realized within seconds that my body wouldn't let me.

I gave my head a shake and held out my hands in front

of me as a pulsing awareness wrapped itself around my arm growing all the way up toward my shoulder.

I quickly jerked out of my button-down black shirt and threw it to the ground.

"Weeellll…" Mason gulped, his skin growing pale. "At least we know it's growing at a more rapid rate now."

I opened my mouth again and gave Cassius a helpless stare. He moved Ethan out of the way and approached while I put my hands up to stop him. I didn't want to hurt him, and I had no control over my body, I could just stand there and exist.

"Speak!" Cassius' voice thundered so loud that my ears rang. "Now!"

I shook my head no, because I truly couldn't.

And then he touched my face. Ice pressed against my cheeks as his eyes went completely white and then shockingly red. My red.

"Keeper of souls… guide them," a voice rasped. "Trapped."

Was that me or inside me?

Cassius swayed and then all of his feathers erupted in a frenzy from his back pointing like razors in my direction. It was his version of a kill shot and he wouldn't let me go.

I was a threat.

Somehow.

I was bad.

I'd always known that, though, hadn't I?

This was on me.

I was worthless; it's why I wanted a soul in the first place.

His feathers slowly descended and pressed against my chest. They drew no blood. They didn't even scratch me.

"You protect this body... why?" Cassius demanded another answer.

The voice erupted from within. "Because it has always been mine... loved, I risked..."

Cassius released me in disgust. I'd never realized a demon could feel shame until that moment.

"Greedy fool," Cassius muttered. "You are split in half!"

I looked down.

He muttered a curse. "Not literally!"

I felt a swirl of power behind me. Alex. They were surrounding me because I was the bad guy—again. Hell, and things had been going so well, hadn't they?

I would walk away from them. From this.

This was beyond them. This was bad if it was beyond Cassius.

"Release!" Cassius yelled, shaking the foundation of the earth beneath my feet.

Suddenly I could talk again, even though it felt like I'd been choked from within. "I'll leave."

"Not so fast." Cassius held his massive hand out. "There's an ancient text... older than—well as old as Sariel. You need to read it."

Oh good, we were taking orders from his dead archangel father now. Perfect.

"So reading it is going to magically cure me from this?" I pointed at my winking tattoo, at the way it pulsed on my arm. And then I just lost it as frustration raged through me. I let out a roar and fell to my knees.

The sun disappeared, immediately followed by the

appearance of clouds of darkness and then a shadowy mist wrapped itself around me.

"Stop calling the shadows!" Cassius gripped me by the arm, then cursed and yanked his hand back. A wicked burn had formed across his palm.

"What the hell did you do, demon?" Alex roared. "Sell your soul to the devil himself?"

"No." Everything felt heavy as I stayed on my knees. "I never had one to begin with."

Cassius's eyes turned silver white as he tasted the air and whispered, "Lie. Try again."

"I don't remember!" I yelled. "Is that what you want to hear? I remember nothing past that day!"

"What day?" This time Mason stepped forward, and repeated himself, "What day?"

My eyes searched Cassius's for help. "I don't know. I just remember begging for it to stop, and she said it would. She said she would make me whole, I was the last of the first, the last of the first," I couldn't stop saying it, "The last of the first."

"Good," Ethan said calmly. "Gibberish from a demon, I don't think any of us signed up for this. Cassius, can't you just mind read him?"

"I… could," Cassius said slowly. "But what if I can't get out, what if it's beyond my power? What if this is something deeper, older, stronger?"

"Can't you find out?" Alex.

Cassius stared us down and then reached for Mason's hand. The apple dropped and rolled toward me and then turned brown and shriveled up to its core.

Power surged between them and hit me square in the chest as I fell backward, my last thought.

Sunshine.

CHAPTER NINE

KYRA

You know those dreams that feel so real that you're upset you've woken up? That's the exact sort of dream that haunted me the entire night, and even when I showed up to work, I couldn't look away from his bright red eyes. They should be terrifying—instead, they just seemed powerful, all knowing. They also seemed… burdened, and I wanted to reach out and grab the face that the eyes belonged to, I wanted to hold it close. Every hard inch of him was godlike in beauty, so much so that I was impressed my imagination could even conjure it up.

I'd been wearing a crown. It was black with enormous rubies. And we danced in a magnificent, colossal ballroom surrounded by so many people, glowing people, people who looked like they belonged on that ridiculous *Hercules* movie from Disney.

Not that I was comparing myself to a Disney princess, because there was something dark and sinister—not bad—but also no longer good about the way people stared at us like they were expecting death to follow.

He was altered in a way that could not be fixed.

I only wished I was a writer so I could pen the story, because it was incredible, and when he pulled me into his arms to kiss me, it felt real.

"I gave my soul for you, sunshine, my everything to have you here with me, in this place. Tell me you don't regret it," he whispered against my mouth. He tasted like darkness, and I soaked in my fill.

"Worth it," I'd promised. Even though I knew our match was cursed before it began, there were rules—we broke them. What was the reason for that? Love? Obsession?

"My beautiful wife—my queen, my sunshine." He bowed before me, earning gasps amongst the crowd. I knew in my soul he never did that—he was the prince of the— prince of the—I squeezed my eyes shut and tried to remember his title.

"Whoa, there!" Tarek slammed into me, his grip on both of my arms. "Any reason you're closing your eyes and attempting to walk at the same time?"

"Uhhh," I gave him a weak smile, "Sorry I just had the craziest dream or vision, I don't even know."

He licked his lips, his glance darted toward the bar and back at me. "Oh?"

"Yeah, I mean it was so vivid, do you ever have those?"

His smile was sad. "I don't really dream."

"What?" I gave him a playful shove. "Everyone dreams. You probably just don't remember them."

He just shrugged and ran a hand through his mop of hair. Huh, he had it down today, it was long, down his back, silky, thick, how did he get away with that and not look ridiculous? "How is that possible?"

"Some of us are born..." He sighed. "Different. Besides, they say that dreams are eight percent reality."

At that, I burst out laughing. "Riiiight, so I married royalty about a billion years ago and here I am, just waiting for my prince to come. Okay."

He clenched his teeth. "You never know, maybe this is your second life. Maybe this is your first and you've just been roaming the world searching for your other half and every time you think you die you just wake up with a new life."

I frowned. "That has to be the craziest and most depressing thing I've ever heard."

He let out a snort. "You're telling me."

"Hey! Can we get some service?" A rude college punk snapped his fingers at me. I instantly wanted to break them off.

"Do it," a voice inside my chest urged.

Um... I looked around and shook it off, reined in my

anger, and walked over to the sad preppy kid with his UW hoody on. "What can I get you?"

"You on the menu?" He high fived his buddy in an identical sweatshirt. Ah great, it was asshole day, lucky me.

"Sorry, I'm married with ten kids. But if you want to be my new baby daddy I'll just need you to pee in a cup and we can go out on our first date with all ten of them. I mean when you marry the mom you marry the kids, am I right?" I fake laughed.

He gave me a horrified look and then grumbled, "Er, yeah, just two Coronas."

I flashed him a purposefully ditzy smile. "Thought so."

The rest of my day was almost identical to that: get hit on, make up a story about kids, and watch the college students rush off toward the other women in the bar who were only too happy to let them make out for hours on end.

Who did that in public?

"Human men," came the answer behind me scaring the crap out of me again as Tarek flashed me a grin. "And some people just like stupid easy prey. Not me though," He leaned in until I could smell his spicy scent. "I like the hunt, live for it, actually."

There was something magnetic about him. I couldn't help but sniff the air—he felt so safe.

The minute I thought it, his face fell. "I ugh, should get back to work."

And then he was gone, leaving me more confused than ever.

"You hurt the pup's feelings." Timber was lurking in the shadows.

"How long have you been standing there?" I crossed my arms, my simple black tank suddenly felt too tight, my jean skirt indecently short as he eyed me up and down slowly only to settle his gaze on my mouth.

He pushed away from the wall and in one graceful stride was right in front of me. "Long enough to know that you have ten kids... or is it seven? You really like to sell numbers to certain guys whereas others you know will give up easy if you just act stupid which you aren't for the record. What I don't understand is why don't you just make up a fake boyfriend? Husband? Why the kids?"

My throat swelled up a bit as I looked down and shrugged. "Kids seem to be the thing that people are too selfish to have. People rarely sacrifice their lives, their love, for someone else and even if they say they will—most wouldn't do it for a complete stranger who works part time at a bar."

He nodded slowly. "That's quite a heavy answer. I was expecting you to say something more along the lines of 'because it works.'"

I smiled at that, "Yeah well, it's been a long day."

"That it has." He suddenly looked exhausted as he reached for my hand. "Shall we?"

"Ah so proper, you taking me into your office to fire me?"

"You should be so lucky to stay away from me, should have run when you had the chance, right out that door, screaming about myths and monsters." His voice lowered and almost snapped as he said it.

I jumped a bit when he opened the door to his office and ushered me inside only to close it with finality and lean against it, once again watching me.

"You smell like sunshine." He said it again like it was irritating him.

I sniffed the air. Smelling nothing but the smell of wood burning and those damn lotus flowers. "Do you need me to change perfumes? Am I getting written up?"

His smile had my knees buckling. "No. And it's not your perfume, it's you."

"Oh awesome, my natural musk smells like sunshine, lucky me!"

"Not so lucky." He said it under his breath as he shrugged out of a black leather jacket revealing a short sleeved black shirt and a tattoo that took over his entire arm.

"Did you just get a sleeve?"

He barked out a laugh. "Yes, and you know what my choices were? A rose and a tree. I just couldn't decide which, soooo why not combine it into a fruit tree with so many branches my eyes get dizzy…"

"Er…" I winced at the unreal black ink. "It's intricate."

"It's a pain in my ass." He shook his head. "Anything peculiar today or are you ready to go home?"

"Home?" I repeated and then checked my watch. "No way! I didn't realize I worked overtime, I'm so sorry. I can—"

He shook his head. I stopped talking.

With a gulp, I pointed behind me. "I'll just be leaving, see you tomorrow."

He stood. "I'll drive, just let me grab my keys."

And that was how for the second night in a row, my very sexy and peculiar boss took me to my apartment, only this time in a jet black Tesla with red seats.

Oddly, it fit him.

I wasn't sure how I knew that, just that it made sense.

We were at my apartment within minutes. I was just about to say thank you when he parked, got out of the car, opened my door, and then escorted me to the front door.

We were silent. My apartment was on the second floor, so we took the stairs, and all the time I wondered what his end game was, my safety or curiosity, or worse, something else?

I finally made it to my door, ready to shove my key in the lock, and nearly passed out when I noticed the door was ajar.

"Son of a bitch." He kept cursing as he shoved the door open, revealing several red eyes staring right back at both of us, all of them belonging to men with gorgeous model like faces, which honestly seemed more out of place then the red eyes.

Maybe they had the wrong apartment?

Maybe they weren't here to...

"Massster." The blond one fell to his knees. "We are at your service."

What. The. Hell.

"We did not know!" Another eyed me nervously, then focused on Timber. "We apologize, we could no longer smell the mark of—"

Timber held up his hand; it was shaking, he clenched it into a fist and then lost his ever-loving shit as he charged the one bowing, kneeing him in the face, kicking him backward and slamming his fist into his jaw. I heard a crack, and then I closed my eyes and plugged my ears—not that it helped, I heard every scream of pain, every broken bone, and then I was surrounded by Timber's scent as he picked me up into his arms and carried me back down the stairs and deposited me into the waiting Tesla.

I was shaking uncontrollably as he pulled out his cell. "Tarek, go to her apartment, let the council know about the bodies." He shot me an apologetic glance. "Have Alex incinerate them—I don't care that they have no souls, they made their choice when they walked in!" He growled out something in another language. "Just do it! I'm taking her to my place, grab her a bag, whatever has her scent on it the most, you take that—" He covered the phone with his hand. "Any valuables you need? Things from your childhood you have stored that you don't want destroyed?"

I opened my mouth, closed it, and then gripped my silver sunshine necklace. "I'm w-wearing it."

"Smart girl," he muttered then barked more orders at Tarek.

He hung up and turned on the heat, then reached across the console and placed his hand on my left thigh, it was bare. I almost jumped anticipating the icy cold of his fingertips, instead they felt warm, they felt soft.

I relaxed a bit, still panicking on the inside.

Still wondering what he meant about incinerate.

After ten minutes, I finally found my voice. "Who were those men?"

Timber wiped a hand down his face and kept driving and then slammed his hands against the steering wheel. "Not human."

Hysterical laughter bubbled up inside me. "Yeah, okay, and you're the abominable snowman!"

The light turned red. He pulled to a stop and gave me

such a menacing look that I leaned back against my door, and then his eyes matched the stoplight, flashing so red that it was impossible to hold the scream in. "No, sweetheart, I'm way worse than that. I am the damned."

I reached for the door handle only to have him squeeze my thigh and hit the accelerator through the rest of the red light. "Struggle and you could die, they have your scent, they want you because you feel warm to them, alive, and if there were that many, it means you've been watched, marked for dead. You stay or you die."

"You, your eyes match theirs." I couldn't take the trembling from my voice or the way my body kept shivering. "They called you 'master.'"

He bit out a curse and turned down a dirt road where I would most likely be killed. Right?

His body convulsed a bit and then he said in a booming voice that caused the car to shake. "I am the last of the first!"

And everything faded to black.

CHAPTER TEN

TIMBER

I paced in front of the couch while Tarek and Mason ate me out of house and home and Cassius stood by the fire deep in thoughts that he refused to share. All I knew? They were bad because his ice kept dousing the fire regardless of what Stephanie did to calm him down.

Genesis and Ethan had been on a rare date night, which I'd interrupted and now I was the focus of both of their glares.

Hope and Alex were seated on the other couch watching Netflix while Serenity stood guard by the door just in case.

It was a complete shit show.

Demons never attacked without my command.

And yet there they'd been, in her apartment, actually hunting a human outside of the clubs.

I wondered if they felt what I did when they touched her. Did they taste colors? Did things finally feel at peace? Or was she just so good they wanted her soul regardless of the laws that were intact—if you wanted yours restored, you could have it, but demons were a selfish race, they wanted what they wanted and they wanted more than one.

We were split down the middle.

I'd like to think I was keeping the peace, and now I was questioning everything.

"Sooooo…" Mason chomped on a piece of raw celery and made a face, "Are we gonna talk about the elephant in the room."

"He means Kyra," Tarek explained, always the helpful one.

"I just want to know what the hell you said to her that made a star actually fall from the sky." Alex grinned at the TV without looking at me.

"Stop exaggerating." I rolled my eyes. "A shooting star bigger than anything in history flew across the skyline toward Egypt, shit happens."

"I love it when the refined sounding ones cuss." This from Mason, which earned a laugh from Ethan.

I groaned into my hands. "Is she at least okay?"

Cassius's eyes flashed white. "She's fine, she's just stunned."

"I mean let's be honest." Alex snorted. "You went full Demon King on her, ohhh, I'm the worst of them all, growl, bite, flash my red eyes, look I have claws. For the love of God tell me you didn't flash a bit of horn, you dirty bastard."

I prayed for patience. "Can someone muzzle him? Huh? Ice him? Cassius, we know you can…"

Ethan chuckled while Alex flipped us all off from his spot on the couch.

"And no." I kept pacing a hole in my carpet. "I didn't go full demon and show her horns," I conveniently left out the part where I hadn't shifted ever since the tattoo started growing, yes my eyes flashed red but I never went into full demon mode at least not anymore and it had been rare once I received my restored soul.

I frowned.

If Hope restored my soul—quite literally my old soul, the one that had been taken from me somehow eons ago—then what sort of used soul had been given to me?

I remembered nothing.

And that was the problem.

"He's thinking too hard," Alex whispered.

I shot him a glare while Cassius locked eyes with me, like he was waiting for me to say something. "What?"

"We can't help you if you don't tell us everything, Timber. You know this and yet you hide the details—one part of you is still living in fear, while the other is attempting to break free, both cannot coexist."

"Thank you, Yoda." I saluted him and ignored the pang in my chest and the pulsing on my tattoo.

Kyra moaned from her spot on the couch.

I rushed to her side, only to have Hope, Serenity, and

Genesis sprint in my direction and huddle over her like moms looking after baby chicks.

"She's stirring!"

"A little less strong." I patted Genesis on the back, "You know, with your mothering."

She gave me a sour look and continued to hover, basically shoving me out of the way while Kyra came to.

"Oh you poor thing!" Hope sat her up. "Do you need food?"

"Water?" Genesis offered.

"Wine, get her wine!" Serenity intervened.

I snorted. "Nobody gave me wine last time I passed out."

"Riiiight," Alex piped up. "Because you destroyed both gardens with your massive body falling onto the grass, so no wine for you, no wine for you ever. If there is ever a family dinner with wine, you get water."

I scowled.

"Still won." Mason chomped on granola bar.

I threw up my hands in exasperation. "Why are you eating all my food?"

He just shrugged.

Werewolves, Watchers, immortals, when would it end?

"Oh!" Kyra jolted up, her eyes taking in the beautiful women surrounding her and the pulsing awareness of the siren sitting a few feet away not to mention a vampire, angels, me, yeah she was in for a rude awakening.

I just had to lose my temper, didn't I?

She pressed a hand to her forehead. "Where am I? There were eyes, red eyes, and so many of them, and then Timber—"

I cleared my throat, so she'd know I hadn't quite disappeared like the nightmare she wanted me to be.

She jerked back like I'd attacked her when I'd saved her, and I'd like to think I was used to that reaction except I wasn't, not from her, not from the girl who made me taste the sunshine in the air for the first time in centuries.

I frowned.

"Your kiss is like life," I whispered against her neck. *"I want you…"*

"We can't." She shuddered against me. "You would have me and lose me."

"It would be worth it."

"The oracle said I would find my soul mate and we would be apart for centuries, always searching, always repeating, until one day, we would make choices and reunite."

I smiled sadly. "What's a few years of searching? When we could have each other now? Enjoy our love now? I would do anything for you?"

And a dark voice whispered in my mind. "Anything, Prince A—"

"Oh you poor thing!" Genesis was in full mom mode, ready to make a pot roast and then lecture me for simply existing. A pulsing headache erupted behind my eyes as I tried to conjure up words that would explain or at least put her at ease.

I looked to Cassius.

I had nothing.

Couldn't he at least *try* to help?

"Kyra, daughter of the sun." Cassius beamed. "You've been touched by both sunlight and by darkness, have you not?"

"Good," I said through clenched teeth. "By all means scare her more!"

"Calm the hell down." Alex stood and went full siren. Well shit. I braced for impact as he turned his attention toward her, but all she did was frown.

Alex tried harder.

Hope burst out laughing. "My favorite day is now this day."

"I'm not working!" Alex looked ready to stomp his foot because he wasn't making her fall into a puddle at his feet.

"Uh, you're working." Tarek started to pant, "Just not on her."

Cassius grinned and watched her closely. "Her soul belongs to another, is owned, by another who searches for her, who has searched for eternities."

My head shot up catching Cassius's gaze.

"I think—" Ethan pushed away from the shadows. "—this is where we tell her a story that doesn't scare her, or at least shouldn't. After all, we're the good guys." He just had to flash a bit of fang.

Kyra let out a scream and clapped a hand over her own mouth.

"Trust me, his bark is worse than his bite," Genesis said helpfully as she pulled down her hair to cover exactly that—his friggin' bite. Only Kyra turned at the wrong moment and caught fang marks.

So far? We weren't really handling the situation well.

How long had it been since we brought a human in? Not long, but all of them had parts of them that were tethered to the immortal world.

Hmmm.

Colors.

Tasting colors.

Sunshine.

"Cassius, try freezing her and see if it works," I offered in a bored tone while I examined my impeccable fingernails.

"The hell is wrong with him?" Alex muttered.

"Aw, does the siren miss sex?" I teased.

He lunged.

Cassius stood between us and moved toward Kyra. "We would never hurt you, though this is a lot to take in, I just want to… touch you. May I do that?"

I almost rolled my eyes. So damn polite.

I could be polite. Right?

Maybe.

I searched my brain for moments when I'd been polite to her and only came up with the time I walked her home and didn't suck her soul from her body. So far? I was losing.

Kyra gulped and looked to me. I nodded slowly and by some miracle it worked.

"Yes," she whispered. "You can touch me." She held out her shaking hand. Cassius took it, and an immediate wall of ice hit all of us at the same time. All except Kyra; her hand seemed to glow—no, it seemed to heat up against his.

Cassius jerked away and then laughed to himself. "I think I might enjoy this."

"Come again?" I hissed.

He just looked back at me and shrugged. "Remember you have choices to make, demon, don't make the wrong one or you may miss out on a grand adventure."

"D-demon?!" Kyra shrieked.

I squeezed my eyes shut. "Thanks, Cassius, really, thank you for just shoving my corpse under the bus and camping an elephant right on top of it for good measure."

"Huh, I was thinking more dinosaur, but sure, yeah what he said." Alex shrugged. "Let's go, Hope. Things to do… in the bedroom."

One by one, they shuffled out leaving me alone with Kyra and Tarek, both of whom looked at me like I was the problem when all I wanted was to be the solution.

"Tarek!" I barked. "Get her some dinner."

"Yes master, right away master," Tarek said in an amused voice. "Should I cook it or just make it raw the way demons feed."

I was going to kill him later.

Kyra yelled again.

"He's joking," I said lamely, earning a petrified stare from her. "And…" My throat all but closed up. "You're safe from me, from all of them, you're… safe." It needed repeating.

"You're a demon. An actual evil demon?" She spat the word.

I hated how much it made me defensive, but hadn't it always? I was more than that, I was more… what the hell was I?

Frustration hit me on all sides as I paced again in front of her.

My memories were not my own. Or were they?

I fought with the very real vision of darkness crawling its way across the hardwood floor like smoke swirling toward us.

If I wasn't actively conjuring up the darkness, it begged the question, who or what the hell *was*?

I stared down as Kyra's eyes widened. She pulled her legs to her chest and trembled. "Please tell me I'm hallucinating."

How was I supposed to tell her I was on the good side of things when shadows were at that very moment revealing themselves to her?

"Not hallucinating," I said in a gravelly voice, and then because I was pissed that she was looking at me in fear, I did, in fact, go full demon and shriek in a booming voice. "Be GONE!"

A flicker of gold snapped from my fingertips like lightning, so brief and swift that I thought I'd imagined it. Only when I looked at my fingertips, they were touched with black like I'd burned from the inside out.

There wasn't pain, but I knew in that moment, using whatever power was inside this body, inside the soul fighting to get free, came at a cost.

Because I felt the tattoo slither across my chest and winced when I looked at my left arm and saw another branch wrap around my wrist like I was going to be buried in a tattooed prison.

Kyra whimpered. "I'm scared."

I let out a sigh and locked eyes with her. "That makes two of us."

CHAPTER ELEVEN

KYRA

His blond hair looked soft, his blue eyes so penetrating that I couldn't look away even though I was petrified. It was all too much, not because I didn't believe it.

Quite the opposite actually.

My parents were obsessed, and I do mean obsessed, with mythology to the point that they made me visit both Greece and Egypt every year. The odd part was that we only ever went to the same places.

And when I asked why we kept repeating the trip the look on their faces was always the same.

Helpless and fearful.

I exhaled softly, not sure how much to say or what to do. Obviously I couldn't go back to my apartment, not with demons lurking. Then again, wasn't that was Timber was?

Part of me wanted to call my mom to say something had happened, but what would that even accomplish other than telling her that all the mythological stories they read me growing up were partially right?

"I think—" My voice didn't sound as shaky as I thought it would. "You should start talking."

Timber's eyes narrowed. "You're not screaming."

"Would it make you feel better?"

He smirked, just slight enough to catch it before sobering. "If it was my name, absolutely, but if it was shrieking and then beating me with a pillow, probably not so much."

"I'd probably use something sharper."

"Noted." He sat down on the couch while Tarek sounded like he was beating pots and pans in the kitchen. What made that much noise to cook? Wrangling a live cow?

"So…" I was afraid to touch him, to sit too close. "You're a demon."

"We're just gonna rip that band-aid right off." He hung his head, and for the first time since knowing him, he seemed, not just uncertain, but ashamed.

I reached out and slid my hand onto his thigh, I don't know why I did it, but I had this compelling need to touch him, to comfort him.

He tensed and then instantly relaxed as he placed his hand over mine and squeezed.

As if things couldn't get any weirder, something flashed in my line of vision, Timber smiling, wearing some sort of Egyptian-looking hat, and gold so much gold, it was everywhere.

"Find me," he whispered.
"Find us," I'd whispered right back.
And then pain, so much pain, like my heart was being ripped in two.

"Are you okay?" Timber asked softly, "You just paled."

"No." I frowned. "Yes. I don't know. I've always had very insane dreams like I've lived another life or maybe just watch way too much TV."

"It's probably the first." He wasn't helping. "Some of the greatest minds can't even conjure up the shit I've seen."

I scooted closer. "Oh yeah? Like what?"

"Ahhhh, she wants me to scare her more?"

"No *she's* just curious." I rolled my eyes. "Plus I think I'm kind of stuck with you now, aren't I?"

He winced. "Until we can get demons to stop hunting you, figure out why you smell like sunshine, and why I can literally taste colors when I'm around you, yes. Stuck."

"You taste colors?"

"Not… usually," he said slowly, his blue eyes blinking up at me. "But with you, it's like I can taste and feel everything, which you should know, for a demon is basically like being given the best gift." He shuddered. "Demons aren't born, they're made, a race that was once the Creator's greatest army, cursed to roam the earth they tried to take over, tried to destroy."

"Wait!" My mind was reeling. "I thought demons were fallen angels."

He shrugged. "Some are, but that wasn't always how it was. The angels see what the price is for insubordination, and all they have to do is take a peek at our lives, what it's like to be without a soul, without ever feeling satiated or full, and they shudder to think of the day where they want forever and are never free."

My throat clogged up as I watched pain flicker across his face. "You mean you're never full? Ever?"

"Just like liquor doesn't do the trick, nothing works, and after centuries of being this way you just get used to being in constant pain. It becomes your companion right along with bitterness."

"I'm sorry."

"You shouldn't be," he said quickly. "Because I asked for this. I just don't remember what caused me to seek it." He stopped himself. "To ask for this curse, some nights I wonder if I was tricked, other times I remember myself begging for a soul so I could just feel *something*—anything, and then when I was given one, I felt it all, including the person's last terrified vision of me as I devoured her whole, so don't be sorry. I am the monster you fear. Don't romanticize what isn't there, Kyra."

My stomach clenched. "Devoured?"

"Eat," he clarified. "I consumed her blood, sucked her

soul from her cold lifeless corpse, and I killed her so I could live."

I was shaking, I couldn't help it. Timber scooted away like he knew I needed space and then sighed. "I know you want to ask if it was worth it, to borrow someone's soul, to finally feel full, to feel whole. It wasn't. I didn't know at the time but you can't just steal a soul that doesn't fit. That's not how creation works, so it was a cruel trick of the goddess I sought out. I would have a worthless soul in my body with memories of torture and terror, and I would still be a monster. It wasn't until Hope, the last remaining Elf princess—" I sucked in a sharp breath. "—started restoring my race that I've felt even an ounce of peace." He looked down at the tattoo wrapping around both of his hands now.

"I feel like you're leaving part of the story out," I whispered.

He didn't look up. "Why's that?"

I gulped. "Everyone is walking on eggshells here. They look at you like you're dying and they can't fix it, and minutes ago that tattoo was only on one hand."

He choked out a humorless laugh. "Caught that, did you?"

"I know we barely know each other..." I whispered. "Maybe talking will help?"

"Talking makes it true," he snapped and then stood and paced in front of me. "The tattoo started growing a few days ago, after one of my nightmares, a memory actually, and when I met you, it..." He stopped talking.

"It what?"

He crossed his arms and faced me. "It grew."

"Grew?"

"I didn't stutter."

"How?"

He gave me an annoyed look. "The brightest immortals in the realm are in this house, and even they don't know. Angelic power doesn't even know—or maybe Cassius does and he just refuses to interfere, damn angels and their inability to do anything except watch."

I gaped. "A real angel?"

He gave me another sigh of annoyance. "In this very house, we met the Vamp, you saw the fangs, an angel, a dark one—both human and angel, a goddess, an elf, a werewolf turned angelic Watcher, long story don't ask, and…" His lips turned into a thin line. "A fluffy puppy."

"Heard that." Tarek growled as he came back into the room with a turkey panini and the largest glass of wine I'd ever seen. "Eat up!"

I narrowed my eyes at him. "You're a dog?"

"Real cool, Timber, make me look like the sad puppy one more time and I'm biting you in the ass—literally."

Timber rolled his eyes. "You'd like it too much. I have a fabulous ass."

"The fact that you stare at your own ass depresses me." And then he eyed me. "You'll have to forgive him. It's been at least a thousand years since he's been laid."

I didn't miss Timber's wince.

Or the sexual tension that erupted around us.

"Okay…" I cleared my throat. "So for the record, you're not an actual dog."

"Werewolf." Tarek grinned and then shrugged. "But if you want to get technical, Mason, my brother, is the King of the pack and of the earth, watches over all the shitty little humans, no offense."

I held up my hands. "None taken."

"Anyway, anyone want to watch a movie?"

"Dibs!" Mason came barreling into the room. "She has to watch *King Lion*!"

Tarek groaned.

"Nope," Serenity followed him, had they all just been eavesdropping? "She's had a stressful day. She gets to watch *Beauty and the Beast*. Plus…" She eyed Timber "It might help her be more understanding."

Timber gritted his teeth. "I'm nothing like the beast!"

"Grumpy, yells more than he should and has poor manners, hmm…" Serenity tapped her fingers against her mouth while Timber mumbled something under his breath and sat down again.

I was starving, so I let everyone bicker while I ate and tried to wrap my head around all the information.

Slowly but surely Timber seemed to relax as he rolled up the sleeves to his black button-down shirt, revealing powerful forearms and the gorgeous inky branches as they seemed to pulse around his body almost imprisoning them in their chaotic beauty.

Someone turned the volume up on the TV, grabbing my attention. The rose in the glass case lost another petal. I'd always hated that part of the story, like some sort of countdown. I remember crying about it when I was little. My mom had to console me with cookies, and when I finally did calm down enough, she said that love surpassed time and one day I would understand what that meant, that even the magic of the rose couldn't keep Belle away. And if anything it was just a reminder that time was running out and that you should tell those you love that you love them the minute you feel it, and say it often.

I smiled at the memory. Both my parents were a bit odd, but I remembered that day fondly because it was one of the first days my mom had made me believe in something bigger than myself.

I sighed and looked over at Timber's arm.

And then I thought about what he'd said, his nightmare triggered something and now it was growing at a rapid pace, I obviously wasn't helping.

And then it hit me!

"IT'S JUST LIKE THE MOVIE!" I shouted, earning everyone's attention as I jumped to my feet and then grabbed his arm.

He hissed out a curse and then smiled sadly at me. "I wish that was true, that I just need someone to love me and all will be well, this isn't a Disney movie, Kyra. Remember, I'm the monster not the prince."

The sadness in his voice almost undid me as I knelt in front of him. A memory blossomed, one so fuzzy I couldn't focus, and it had me almost dizzy.

I'd done that before.

I'd knelt for this man before.

My eyes shot to his. Golden flecks pressed through the blue of his irises, and then the red overtook again.

I ran my hand down his forearms and shook my head. "I could be wrong, but I think, I think the tattoo is a countdown."

Behind me, Tarek chuckled. "To what? His death? The end of the world?"

Timber went completely still and whispered. "Cursed to repeat until the souls find one another, cursed in a prison of darkness and shame for daring to take what wasn't mine. Cursed." He swayed forward and then in a voice that sounded eerily familiar whispered. "Find. Me."

CHAPTER TWELVE

TIMBER

Egypt

"*I*t isn't done!" *A booming voice pierced through the darkness, through my morose thoughts as I paced down the gold hall.* "*You know what will happen to you! You will lose everything, brother! Everything!*"

I slammed my fists against his golden armor shoving him against the nearest pillar. "*She's worth it.*"

"*No.*" *His face was filled with sadness.* "*Don't make this* choice. We were supposed to rule together. You're choosing her over an eternity!"

"I'm choosing love," I snapped, shoving him away and giving him my back, something I had never done in a thousand years. "I'm tired of this, we're better than this, brother. Let me be happy."

"Your happiness," he whispered. "At what cost? You know what it will force me to do. You know I will hunt you. I will kill you, he will stop at nothing."

I smirked. "You can try. It isn't easy killing something immortal."

"No, but there are some fates..." His eyes flashed red. "... worse than death."

"That isn't your call to make. The Creator—"

"Has given us free rein." He sneered. "We are the last of the first." His voice boomed. "And I will die a thousand deaths, suffer an eternity in Tartarus before I see you gone from this realm, find another way, I beg you."

"I've made my choice," My voice cracked.

"I know. You, dear brother, are already damned."

"Hey!" Kyra was waving a hand in front of my face. "Are you okay? You just transported somewhere mentally."

How long had I even been out?

Cassius was standing to her side, his expression grim, which I could never tell if that was a good or bad sign, since the guy rarely smiled. "Tell me what you did."

"I sat down," I said slowly. "And then had a very odd vision, where I was wearing armor made out of—"

"Gold." Kyra finished on a whisper.

My head jerked in her direction. "How did you know that?"

Hands shaking she gave me a panicked look. "I've seen it in my dreams."

Cassius cleared his throat next to us. "Kyra, why did you walk into Timber's bar for a job?"

She gave me a blank stare and then shook her head. "My parents decided to move back to Greece, and I wanted to stay. They suggested bartending when I needed money, and my mom mentioned one of her favorite places was Soul."

"And your parents?" Cassius asked softly. "What do they do for a living?"

Why did it matter? I was about to say as much, when Kyra licked her lips and answered.

"Historians, they're historians."

"What sort of history?" Cassius just wouldn't relent, and the room dove a few degrees as frost appeared in front of his face.

"All history, but they used to go on and on about—" She shook her head. "I'm going to sound like an idiot, but they used to go on and on about the Greek gods."

Cassius smiled. "Did they, now?"

"It was a hobby," she said quickly.

"Call them." He handed her his cell phone, weird that he even had one but whatever. "Right now."

"What?"

"Cassius." I groaned. "Get there faster."

"I'm testing something. Call them. Now. Please." He rarely said please, and maybe he *was* on to something. It was better than sitting there hating that she was sighing at *Beauty and the Beast*, because she knew the happy ending, and only a silly mortal would believe that it could ever be my reality, or hers for that matter.

I felt the need to reassure her, to put my arm around her and tell her that Cassius was just being demanding as usual, and part of me hated the false hope I felt that maybe I would get an answer.

"Okay." Kyra took the phone typed in the numbers then put it on speaker, after three rings a sleepy female voice answered. "Mom?"

"Honey? What's wrong? Are you okay? Whose phone is this?"

"Um…" Kyra eyed Cassius.

Huh, what a question. She was in the presence of immortals and getting twenty questions from an angel. No, she wasn't *okay*.

"She's fine," I answered for her.

The phone went silent and then. "What was that?" Not who, what.

I frowned. How would she know based on my voice?

"That was Timber." She gulped. "My boss."

Could I sound any more boring? No, the answer was no.

"I'm confused. Why are you calling, honey? You're worrying me. And that man sounds… unsafe."

She had no idea.

Cassius cleared his throat. "Actually, we're the ones that are worried, it seems your daughter knows something or maybe doesn't know she knows it, and I think that it's time you tell her exactly what she is."

Her mother gasped. "Who are you?"

Cassius shared a look with Kyra before saying in an authoritative voice. "I'm so glad you asked, I am the King of the Immortals, and I demand you tell us everything." He said it so calmly, so matter-of-factly, I almost barked out a laugh. Cassius never did things in half measures, did he?

Another gasp, and then what sounded like hushed voices before a male voice joined, I assumed her father. "So it's true then?"

"You'll have to be more specific." Cassius said. "Is it true we exist or is it true that you know more than you've let on?"

Her mother sighed heavily. "It's been a very long journey for our family with secrets we've been forced to carry for years."

I eyed Kyra, confusion marred her vision, as if she didn't understand the answer.

Cassius's eyes chose that moment to go completely white as he nodded his head. Great, we were going to get the creepy voice, in three, two, one. Ah, there it was. "How many years has Kyra been reborn?"

The father cursed. "Millennia, centuries, nobody knows exactly, time is a fickle thing, you know that, don't you?"

"And your job? To search for what?" Cassius prodded while Kyra wrapped her arms around her body, I'd never seen a person look more frail, so I did what any idiot with a brain would do, I jerked her against my chest and held her there.

It didn't matter that I was darkness and she was light.

It didn't matter that I probably didn't deserve to even touch her, or that she calmed me more than I calmed her. Hell, I was probably making it worse, but I couldn't just stand there. What mattered was that no matter what you are made of, you are still in possession of a heart, of a soul, of something that makes you recognize when someone needs you and because the Creator is in everyone—you are compelled to respond. So respond, I did.

What I didn't account for, was the way she felt pressed against me, or the way her small hands inched around my body hugging me as I shielded her from words that seemed so much more powerful than a punch.

I held on tight.

And then I kissed her head, wondering what the hell had come over me as Cassius waited for the answer I wasn't sure we were going to get.

And finally, her father said, "It was always passed down, our family secret, that one day she would be reborn and finally find her other half, that the curse would be broken, and each time someone in our family got pregnant it was only ever one child, a girl, with dark hair and hypnotic eyes, and every time her life was cut short, only to have history repeat itself. I woke up a month ago and heard it as clear as day, a voice said it was time, and then I dreamed of Soul of a man with white hair and red eyes, so we took our chances."

Rage filled me as I snapped. "You took her chances with demons? Are you insane!" Blood surged through my system as I tried to regain control of my emotions. "Do you have any idea the danger you put her in! Someone has marked her as fresh meat! Had I not been there, demons would have fed on her innocent soul!"

"Timber," Cassius warned.

"No!" I roared. "Don't reprimand me. What they did

was wrong! She could have died and I will not live another century this way!"

All eyes turned to me as my chest heaved. Kyra looked up at me in confusion, something flickered in her gaze, maybe I imagined it, maybe not, but I could have sworn I saw gold.

"Centuries?" Her father's voice interrupted. "Who said that?"

"We'll take it from here." Cassius said in a gruff voice, hanging up the phone and sliding it into his pocket, giving me a curious look that said everything and nothing all at once. Perfect. "It's been a long night, get some rest."

Seriously? That was it?

I opened my mouth to say something then felt Kyra again, the heat of her touch as it nearly singed my clothing, my skin, and suddenly all I wanted was sleep.

"Sure." I found myself saying, "Right." Sleep. Sleep was good.

"We'll just be going." Cassius said cryptically as he ushered everyone out of my house, everyone but Tarek.

I frowned when Tarek gave me a smug look then pointed at the door everyone had just walked out, "I'm gonna go for a drive, be back in a few. Oh, and some pointers, not that you need any, but… be nice."

"I *am* nice," I snapped.

He nodded. "Sure… like a grumpy piranha. Don't bite, that won't help anything. Oh, and just… go with it."

"With what?" I was exhausted, confused, but she was so warm.

"Mine," a voice hissed.

Tarek shut the door, and we were alone.

Me and the girl who feared me, great what could possibly go wrong?

"Um." Five. The amount of times I'd uttered that word in my entire existence, what the hell was happening to me? "Do you need to shower or…" My throat went dry. I was still holding her, she wasn't pulling away.

"No." She shook her head. "Just point me to a bed, and I'll be okay."

I didn't like that. Her alone in a room even though my house was safe, I just didn't like it, because it physically hurt.

Actually, everything hurt.

Worse than usual.

Wasn't the soul supposed to help the burning pain in my stomach as it sizzled and snapped.

I clenched my free hand and winced.

"What's wrong?" She grabbed my hand before I could pull it away, more branches swirled around my arms. It felt like I was being buried alive.

I didn't panic but something or someone inside me did.

I had the urge to yell no.

To fight it.

But I had no idea what it was.

So I lied. "I'm fine, just tired."

"Oh." She frowned. "Okay."

I gave myself a mental slap and forced a smile I hoped wasn't too predatory as I pointed to the hall. "I'll just show you your room."

She fell into step beside me as we made our way down the dark hall and to the first guest room on the right. Something settled in my chest, almost like I could finally take a deep breath as we stepped over the threshold into the room.

I'd painted it in calming blues with brown accents, a leather chair and a flat screen were on the left, and a huge four post king bed was opposite.

"What the hell?" She stopped and looked up at me. "That's creepy, even for you! How did you do it? How?"

"What?"

She gave me a shove, clearly not afraid of me anymore. I think I liked it better when she was giving me hugs. "You know!"

"I truly don't and stop yelling!" I snapped, my fangs gleaming at her, too far, too aggressive. Shit.

"You're yelling, you psychopath!"

"I am not," I took a few deep breaths and growled, "a psychopath!"

"Oh, I'm sorry." She looked anything but. "Just a really good stalker? Who went to my parents' house? You? Tarek? Creepy Cassius?!"

I burst out laughing. "Oh, I can't wait to tell him his new nickname."

She shoved me again. It tickled. "I'm serious!"

"What's with the sudden violence?" I roared. "I have no clue what you're talking about!"

"This!" She spread her arms wide.

I gaped. "The room?"

"Yes the room. What else would I be pissed about?"

"Er... my existence?" I offered helpfully. "You're the one shouting."

"Because!"

"Great answer." I rolled my eyes "Women."

"Maybe you'd get laid more if you understood them!"

"Said that last part slow for my benefit, did you?" I glared.

"Timber, be serious."

"This is me," I said as calmly as I could, "being serious. I have no idea why you're throwing a—"

Her eyes narrowed.

"—Perfectly normal fit over the color blue."

"Better," she muttered. "Timber, this is identical to the room I grew up in. And when I say identical I mean, when I graduated high school I got a brand new white faux fur rug for the room," She pointed down to the rug. "That one, right there."

I frowned. "That's impossible."

"Clearly not!"

"It's impossible," I said through clenched teeth. "Because this room has always been blue, I've always had this bed, and until recently nothing has changed except for the damn rug and the TV!"

Her body jerked. "When did you buy the rug and TV?"

"Let me just go find my receipt I kept from three years ago and give you the exact date, you crazy human!"

Not my best choice in words.

She gasped.

I got slapped.

And my cheek was still stinging when she muttered, "Three years?"

"Three years."

"Three years ago, I graduated college, moved back home, and updated my room."

"Does that make us twins?"

"Timber!"

I sighed. "It's a coincidence."

"Nothing about us is an accident!" she fired back.

And I knew I couldn't disagree, I just didn't understand, and if I was being completely honest, no part of me felt worthy to.

"Right, well..." My control was slipping as red lined my vision. "...it feels like it is. Just a horrible accident that was never meant to happen in the first place. Where a man cursed meets the only person in existence who makes him feel—and she was meant for someone else."

I was talking about the other soul then inside me screaming. The one that wanted her more than anything, and the very real demonic nature that kept tapping it down, silencing it.

I felt pain again. Searing pain in my vision, and again in the palms of my hands.

Trapped in another prison, watching while whatever inside me suffered for her touch.

Knowing it was him she wanted.

Not me.

"Kyra, I'm sorry."

"What? What are you sorry for?"

"I'm sorry that whatever needs you, loves you, calls for you inside me, will never show itself. I'm sorry that I'm not strong enough to remember, I'm sorry that the face that you see isn't the face you want nor the face you deserve. I'm sorry, that this most likely won't be a happy ending but another tragedy."

She was silent and then. "What makes you think it's not you that I want? You that my soul needs?"

"I have lived for millennia Kyra, one thing has always remained true. The demon, does not win."

"But—"

"I'm going to bed."

"Timber."

"Goodnight." I shut the door and walked away before I did something stupid like ask her to touch me again, ask her to tell me that she wanted *me*, not whatever was inside me, calling to her.

Power surged through me.

And out of pure anger, I hushed it with a hiss and whispered, "At least let me have a day with her before you take over."

I didn't think I would get an answer.

Instead, a dark chuckle filled my ears and then a hoarse whisper. *"Remember."*

CHAPTER THIRTEEN

KYRA

I stared at the closed door in frustration. He was hiding something. Then again I had been too, not about anything paranormal or as freaky as he was—but the fact that I knew there had always been something off about my parents, about the looks they gave me, the moments they would hold my hand as if one day my life truly would be cut short and they would be left with ash.

Frustrated, I walked over to the bed and sat. It was more

comfortable than mine back at my parents' old house; at least the brand wasn't identical.

Why would this room look like mine?

Why would it even matter in the grand scheme of things other than for my own personal comfort in prison?

A demon's prison.

I shivered.

I didn't understand my response to him, just like he didn't seem to understand his response to me; it was almost like instinct. Logically, I wanted to pull away from what I perceived as danger.

But in my soul something stirred when I saw him, like a memory from long ago, like the dreams that always drip into nightmares that feel too real to bear.

Maybe I'd wake up and this would be just that, like *Inception*, maybe someone was planting an idea.

I pinched my arm. Sharp, stinging pain radiated outward.

Yeah, this was real.

Too real.

I yawned behind my hand and lay back against the pillows, I wasn't tired, but my eyes felt heavy as I reached for my silver sunshine necklace and twisted it in my fingertips.

The last thing I remember.

Was the smell of cedar and ash…

"The solstice," I whispered. My nerves were completely frayed. I was wearing a ball gown that reminded me of sunshine—reminded me of my father who was at this very moment in a terse conversation with my mother as they sat on the two horses in front of us.

We were getting closer.

The smell of ash mixed with ambrosia was getting worse.

I was going to be sick.

Maybe not sick, but my stomach was rolling in waves that reminded me of home.

A place I wouldn't return to for a very long time. Then again, that was what happened when your father was desperate.

A soul for a soul.

A life for a life.

In order for our people to not just survive but thrive, we needed this alliance. The rumors hadn't been kind.

Then again, I doubted the gods cared.

Sand swirled in front of us, and like a mirage, huge white stone buildings suddenly appeared in front of us. Jewels shone inside the rocks, and flowers fell from some unseen place in the sky.

People cheered all around us as a team of soldiers led our horses into the inner gate.

The palace was bigger than I imagined. It was ten times the size of the Prince of Egypt's residence.

Ten. Times.

I shivered as a chill wracked my body.

There he was, in all his godlike beauty, standing in the center of it all. My betrothed.

The man I would marry.

Two countries would align.

The only price?

My virginity.

King Set gave me a peculiar look then leered over his shoulder. I followed his gaze and nearly fell off my horse.

He stood at least nine feet tall.

Clouds appeared out of nowhere, covering the sunshine, filling the air with ash as the creature slowly made its way toward us. With the head of a jackal and the body of a man, he moved painfully slow until he was near my horse, towering over it actually.

"Are you afraid?" His red eyes flashed.

I gulped. "If I say no you'll know I'm lying, if I say yes I'll insult the gods, what would you have me do, dark prince?"

"You know me by name why not use it?" he hissed.

"I'm not worthy to utter it to his Highness's face."

He inclined his head, and then he was lifting me, his massive hands were hot against my hips as he lowered me to the ground. "You know what happens next."

"If I survive, yes."

His beastly face didn't as much as blink, the gold armor covering part of his head shone even though the sun had run away from his mighty presence.

And then he very slowly pressed a hand to my chest. It felt like I might be split in half as he pulled something airy and blue from my skin, twisting it this way and that and then pressing it back into my chest again. "King Apollo doesn't lie. His daughter is pure of soul and of body."

King Set grinned at me menacingly, I didn't realize what I was doing, but I'd actually hidden behind the god, the god we were not allowed to touch, not allowed to even be near.

It was a slight brush of my fingertips along the line of his warm skin.

He stilled.

And very slowly said under his breath. "Worthless."

"Sorry."

"I wasn't talking about you." His eyes were on *King Set, rumored to be a god himself though he never revealed his beast. I wondered what it would be, what form he would take, then again, they were nothing but rumors*

The gods had long ago abandoned us.

All save three.

Choosing to reveal themselves only when necessary—while the rest were imprisoned for altering the human race.

It was a price punishable by death.

Intervention.

I hung my head as the truth settled on my shoulders. I would give my virginity to this man, and even this dark prince could not, would not prevent it.

I moved around him and very slowly made my way up the white marble stairs, each step felt heavier and heavier, until I stopped in front of the massive King.

He had jet black hair, crystal blue eyes, and a smile that was menacing in a way that promised pain, not pleasure.

I bowed low. "King Set."

"I think you'll enjoy your time here, princess."

Protection. My country needed protection. The times of old were ending, we needed more than an army—we needed the favor of the gods.

I swallowed the dryness in my throat and then met his gaze. "The pleasure is all mine."

He smiled. "Oh, it will be. Trust me."

My stomach rolled.

Darkness followed me as the jackal moved to the King's right side and stood.

"Son?" King Set said. "You've measured and found her pure?"

"I have."

"She stays that way. She's mine." King Set's voice boomed.

The jackal tilted his head at me then snapped his fingers, a black mist filled the air and then the head of the beast was gone and in its place...

Utter perfection.

Full lips, strong jaw, muscle on top of muscle, with white blond hair that hung in loose braids with jewels twined through them. His eyes were bright blue, and the gold of his armor was almost blinding.

"You'll have to forgive my son." King Set grinned. "He may be the envy of every male and female in the realm for his beauty, but his words are few."

I nodded just as King Set placed a hand on my lower back pulling me forward and whispering, "Tonight."

I woke up in a pool of my own sweat, and with a red-eyed demon hovering over me like I'd somehow conjured him in my sleep.

"Seriously!" I shoved him. "As if I'm not scared enough now, I have to worry about you watching me sleep!"

He scowled. "I heard you scream, so I ran. And the last person who woke me out of my slumber is missing his spleen, so I would choose your next words carefully."

"A spleen." I repeated as his red eyes narrowed at my sweaty state. "Why a spleen?"

"Easy, they taste better."

I gasped. Horrified. Absolutely horrified. Only to earn a small smirk from Timber, who shrugged.

"You're making fun of me."

"Naturally." He stood and walked over to the black dresser. "The spleen was easier to grab and I was standing in front of this person, so I just reached, twisted, and—" He looked over his shoulder with a grin. "Popped."

"I will never think of popcorn the same way again. Ever."

"Ah the sound of popcorn, not unlike the sound of skin as it—"

I held up my hand. "If this is your way of scaring me more than my nightmares, do please continue!"

He rolled those gorgeous blue eyes in my direction and then threw a plain white shirt in my direction followed by a pair of black boxers. "Change."

"Now?"

Timber looked around. "Did I need to schedule it in or something?"

"You're a smart ass."

"Why, thank you." He winked. "Just change so you don't smell like sweat and nightmares. You'll feel better, in fact," He held up a hand and then walked into the adjoining bathroom, and the sound of water filled my ears.

I jerked.

Water.

Dripping.

Cleaning.

Blood.

"He hurt me," I whispered. "I didn't know…"

"He's drunk." Large hands helped me to my feet. "Cover

yourself up, and I'll talk to my brother. Perhaps both of us could... intervene."

"No!" I gripped him by the armor forgetting my own nakedness. "You can't, you'll be punished, I'll be punished, my family won't survive—"

"It will be fine," he said smoothly. "Am I not powerful?"

"You are."

And then he leaned in and murmured, "The first of the last, the last of the first."

"Timber." I felt my body sway.

He was at my side in an instant. "What is it?"

"The water... do you ever have dreams where you're not watching it happen but experiencing it?"

He was quiet and then, "Yes. Nightly."

"This man," I said, pushing through the hoarseness in my voice. "He's in my dreams now, and bear with me when I say this, but he has the head of a jackal—" Timber jerked away, his eyes haunted, his stance rigid, angry.

"Go on."

"In my nightmare, he tested my soul, to see if it was pure, and then I was in front of King... King Set and he was leering at me, and I had no choice because—"

"The gods do not intervene," Timber finished sadly. "You must be very old indeed, Kyra if that's you."

"I don't think it's me. I think it's maybe old me, and reborn me just gets to see shadows of her horror and abuse."

Timber hung his head and then, "Shower and we can discuss."

"I want to discuss now," I snapped as tears filled my eyes.

"Sorry, I'm just… you turned on the water and I was there again, in seconds, staring up at the man—"

"The jackal?"

"He turns into a man whenever he wants. He's…" My cheeks heated.

Timber let out a low growl. "Do not finish that sentence if you value your life."

"Threatening me doesn't help."

"Jealousy makes me want to rip limbs from bodies."

I frowned. "You're jealous of a man who no longer exists."

"I'm jealous of anyone who has touched you and tasted what I taste. I'm jealous of anyone who experiences life to its fullest, warmth of a good woman with a good soul, when I know I'm damned to Hell, so yes, I'm jealous."

I swallowed the lump in my throat. "I'm sorry."

"Don't be." He sighed and then joined me on the bed. "I'll remember that running water is a trigger, and until then," He placed a hand on my thigh. "I think I may have a minor solution."

I stared down at his hand, the black branches covering his skin swirling with madness across his thumb and forefinger. Pulsing with an energy that seemed to be doing its hardest to keep whatever was inside him.

In.

"What's your minor solution?" Darkness chose that inopportune moment to just slither across the bedroom floor. I lifted my feet to the bed and shuddered.

Timber stared it down then looked up at me, his red eyes flashing. "Don't fear the darkness. Often times the evil resides in plain sight."

Slowly, I lowered my feet to the ground. The black didn't touch me; it swirled around my ankles but didn't do anything except for exist. "What is it?"

"If I told you, you'd think you'd lost your mind."

"Try me."

"Remnants of the underworld, shadows that take souls."

I lifted my legs again. "Just to be sure."

Timber cracked a smile. "The darkness has to ask permission to take any living thing, so to you it's harmless."

"And what about you?" I wondered out loud.

He sighed heavily. "Part of me thinks it's waiting," He pressed a finger to the middle of his palm where the seed had taken root. "Waiting for the day this covers me whole, waiting to finally take my borrowed soul and my restored soul to a place of final rest."

"What happens if the darkness pulls the borrowed soul first?" I wondered.

"I imagine that my restored soul, the one given to me by the Creator, would stay imprisoned in this body while the borrowed one finally got rest. Not the happiest ending to the story but at least the woman who died will finally know peace."

"But will you?" I asked.

"Peace." He repeated. "What a magical, nonexistent idea." He turned to me. "This is going to hurt, I'm not a vampire. We don't feed for pleasure. It will sting and you'll want to fight me, but it might be worth trying."

I narrowed my eyes. "What would be worth trying?"

"Blood carries memories, if you're reborn, I can search the older ones and try to put the puzzle pieces together. The only reason I won't be able to do it is if someone or something has purposefully put a block there."

I chewed my lower lip. "Why would anyone or anything want to block a memory? My memories to be specific?"

He was quiet for a few seconds. "Perhaps unleashing what's locked inside is too powerful or a threat. Maybe some things are purposefully kept weak and searching so that those who feel threatened by them remain strong."

The darkness slithered away from us then, back under the door and out of the room.

"Well, that was creepy," I said under my breath.

"Welcome to my world, human." Timber just sighed like he was annoyed he was still living in it, and then pressed my body back against the bed. "Try not to enjoy my touch too much."

I rolled my eyes. "You're good looking but I think I can manage."

"Good looking, wow, easy on the compliments. My ego can't take it."

I scowled. "You know you're attractive. Now, just tell me what to do."

He hovered over me, his body was rock solid his eyes had turned red. "Try not to scream."

"You really, really need to work on your bedside manner," I hissed.

He just shrugged. "Demon. But I can get Cassius if you prefer angel?"

Something in me shouted no. I found myself shaking my head. "No, it needs to be you."

His face softened. "Don't worry human, it's just a bite, and Cassius knows how to draw out the poison."

Every muscle in my body tensed, readied me to flee. "Poison?"

"Skipped that did I?" He winced. "Demon bites don't heal... well. But we have a goddess and an angel, you'll make it, and I won't curse you."

"Was there a time where you were going to?" I asked, unable to keep a note of hysteria from my voice, earning me a rough laugh from the gorgeous man straddling me.

"No," he said in a clear voice. "Never."

"Okay." I licked my lips. "I trust you."

"You shouldn't." He sighed in annoyance, "Yet here we are. Never thought I'd see the day when a human tells the Demon King she trusts him."

"And yet," I said sarcastically, as I repeated his words back at him, "here we are."

"Yes." His eyes roamed my face, landed on my lips, and stayed there as he rasped. "Here we are."

I turned my head and felt his slight movement as his lips grazed down my neck. They felt warm, and that heat increased with each kiss I felt tongue, soft and wet, and then something sharp scraped down my skin.

"Stop teasing your meal," I said in a shaky voice.

"Oh, I don't drink blood to survive," he whispered in my ear. "I eat the body and the soul, no leftovers. The blood just tells me information I need."

"Thanks for clarifying."

"Monster," he reminded me. "Now hold still."

I squeezed my eyes shut as his fangs punctured the left

side of my neck, the pain wasn't unbearable, but it wasn't pleasant either. I held my scream in as his lips drew up against my skin and sucked.

I thought I knew pain.

I was wrong.

This wasn't just pain this was desolation, this was emptiness, and in an instant, my back arched against the bed as the bite took a turn I wasn't expecting.

I hooked my legs behind his body, plastering him against me as his weight pressed me against the mattress, every inch of him covered me suffocated me until I wanted to be consumed by him, wanted to ask if he needed the other side too, the rest of my body.

All of me.

A moan escaped my lips as he growled against my skin, his hands moving to cup my face as his mouth left my neck and found mine.

His kiss tasted like cedar and smoke, my lips were burning from the inside out as his tongue slid inside.

Something snapped between us, I wasn't sure what, but one minute I was on my back the next we were rolling off the bed, landing with a soft thud as his hands went behind my head to break our fall. His mouth, however, never left mine.

Kissing Timber was like experiencing hunger and thirst all at once, only to ever feel satisfied when he kissed me back, giving me small morsels of what I needed, what I would kill to have.

I threaded my hands through his blond hair, then ran them down his arms, the minute my skin touched his tattoo, the spell was broken.

Blisters appeared on my fingertips where the black had touched.

Timber broke the kiss and gripped my hands in his with a frown, careful not to let any part of his tattoo touch my skin. "I don't understand."

His skin took on an unnatural glow almost pulsing beneath the black.

And before my eyes, the tattoo slithered up his neck wrapping around it like a chokehold, stopping just below his chin only to draw slow intricate circles up the sides of his face.

It was beautiful and terrifying.

"What's happening?" I asked in a quiet voice.

"You'll have to be more specific. Are you talking the bite, the kiss, the deeper kiss, or the fact that I'm stuck in a tattooed prison made up of ugly plants?"

Tears filed my eyes. "It's not funny."

"Death never is." He blew across my blistered hands and then sighed. "I'll call Cassius, he'll take care of this."

"And what about you?" I just had to ask.

"I don't think—" He gulped. "—that I'll be a problem much longer."

He started to walk away.

Urgency filled me. "What did you see? In my blood?" I called out.

"The sun," he said seriously. And then he walked off like that was a good enough answer.

I stumbled after him, chased was more like it, and when I caught up, I grabbed him by the shoulder and turned him around. "What does that mean?"

We were in the doorframe, chests heaving for different reasons or maybe just the same one we refused to discuss.

The kiss.

"If I knew," he said hoarsely, "I would tell you."

"And the kiss?" I crossed my arms.

"We got carried away." His jaw flexed before he looked down. "It happens."

"You're too controlled to use that excuse."

With a smirk, he leaned over until he was inches from my face. "And you're what? A demon expert? Or just an expert on self-control?"

"It happened."

"Yes. It did." He pointed at his face. "Clearly. Every time I touch you I get punished, maybe it's a warning sign… not to touch the human that houses the sun."

"The sun's a star, try again."

He snorted out a laugh of disbelief. "Wow. Yes, the sun's a star—also known as Ra."

I gaped at his retreating form. "I'm not housing a god!"

"You're housing his essence," he called over his shoulder. "Trust me, I would know."

"How?"

"Because." His face was shadowed as he turned back around. "I was part of the army that failed at destroying him, and then everything went painfully dark."

"When?"

He smirked. "You weren't even a flicker in the Creator's eye."

"How old are you?"

He didn't turn around just whispered, "I wish I actually knew."

CHAPTER
FOURTEEN

TIMBER

I could have sworn that her blood mocked me when I tasted her and then it changed altogether, I needed more, craved it, felt like I had been imprisoned for millennia waiting for a taste.

My thoughts were dark as I waited for Cassius, and turned even darker when he entered the room with purple spiked feathers pointed at me and a grim expression on his face when he took in the tattoo covering part of my face.

"So, it's spread has it?" He stated the obvious.

"No." I deadpanned. "I just wanted the top to match the bottom. Yes it spread, after we—"

I cleared my throat, Cassius's eyebrows shot up. "Do continue."

I shifted in my leather chair. "After we—"

"Midnight snacks!" Tarek and Mason stumbled through my front door followed by Alex and Ethan.

"I called *you*, not the council," I pointed out in an irritated voice.

"It's ladies' night." Ethan plopped down on my couch, grabbed my remote, turned on my TV. "Plus you look like hell, thought you could use some cheering up."

"Do I get to kill you?" I asked innocently.

"Nope."

"Then consider me less than cheered."

Alex gave me a wave and sniffed the air, then looked at me, then sniffed again, followed by Mason and Tarek. It wasn't convenient that I forgot they could smell lust in the air.

And I was doing a shit job at controlling mine.

Any sane being would have trouble doing so under these circumstances!

She'd responded.

No human woman responded in that way, least of all to me. They felt the danger, and once the haze lifted, they screamed.

She'd kissed me back.

I shifted in my seat and looked up.

Every single male was waiting in silence.

"I bit her," I admitted in a surly tone. "In my defense I

was trying to see if I could gain some information, and if you must know there was a kiss." Several kisses, but they didn't need to know that.

"It smells like sex." Alex pointed out.

"I wish." I grumbled, earning a chuckle from Tarek who was silenced by an angry-looking Mason.

"The tattoo," Mason pointed out, his eyes going feral. "It's not going to stop."

"As always, thank you for your astute observation."

Thank the Creator, Kyra appeared that same minute.

"She's injured." I stood. "Which is why I called Cassius, not the council, *Cassius*, say it with me!"

Nobody spoke.

Kyra gave me a brave smile and then held out her hands palm up while Cassius stared down at them.

It wasn't Cassius that said something though—no, it was Mason.

"Ancient," he whispered in reverence. "The boils are scarring into intricate designs, the magic is…" His eyes widened in horror as he looked up. "Cassius, tell me you chose not to know this, chose not to see the future or the past."

"I chose," Cassius said slowly. "Because as you know, we cannot intervene especially with something this powerful, but I can take care of the wound on her neck and remedy the poison in her veins."

Mason growled and ran his hands through his dark hair. "This isn't…" He gave me a sad look. "I'm sorry."

"Sorry." I repeated. "What are you sorry for?"

"I didn't see it before, maybe I didn't want to," He gently

held out Kyra's hand, "The only thing in existence that can scar or even create a wound from a curse like this, isn't just ancient, it's old magic, older than old. It's not even magic. It's…" He looked to Cassius. "It's from the old gods."

I burst out laughing. "The ones currently serving time in the Abyss. Great, let's just call Zeus. Oh wait, he doesn't exist—"

"Blasphemy!" Cassius roared. "You will not disrespect the old gods in this house. They still listen to the cries of the people they failed. You know as much as I, that the gods are one in the same, Egyptian, Roman, Norse, Greek—all come from one single story, one single power source that the Creator has since snuffed out."

I nodded. "Sorry."

Mason gave me a funny look. "When we met, you had been a demon for a few hundred years. Yet you're older."

Ethan piped up. "He's older than me, and I'm old as hell. He's older than even Cassius, which is saying something…"

"So?"

"It is time," Cassius said in a sad voice. "I can't undo what's been done to her hands, but it is time that you pull back the secrets, the lies, the shame. Tell us, Timber, whose soul do you house? Whose soul screams for release?"

I shook my head. "You're asking me for something I don't remember."

Alex stood and circled me while Kyra watched with obvious fear in her eyes. I would miss that short cropped black hair, the blue streaks that teased me with the play of light.

I was old.

But I would still miss my life.

Even if it was filled with darkness and chaos.

War and more war.

"He said he fought Ra in a war." Kyra said softly.

"See if I tell you any more secrets," I snarled in her direction.

"Your secrets are going to get you killed!" Cassius shouted, his face went ashen. "Ra, you fought Ra. Ethan, grab the book of the gods—"

"What?"

"Do it!"

Ethan went to my library and returned a minute later with the book of the gods.

The very first page should have a list of them, followed by parentage, attributes, abilities.

But when Cassius opened it.

No page existed.

In fact, several pages from the ancient text were missing as if torn and burned, I wouldn't know because we never opened the old texts what use did they have when all of the gods were no longer in existence?

He snapped the book closed. "The choice is yours, demon, you must remember your past, to save your future."

"Be serious." I laughed. "I'm just old, it's why I don't remember, I was created, I was—" I frowned. "I crawled in the sand to the goddess, begged for a borrowed soul since mine had been…" A piercing headache throbbed behind my eyes. "Not taken." I looked up into Cassius's knowing glance. "My soul wasn't taken!"

"No, demon. Your soul was trapped. Cursed." He turned to Kyra, "Just like yours."

"Related?" Ethan asked while Mason paced in front of us.

Cassius just shrugged. "How should I know? There are hundreds of paths, hundreds of possibilities, but no, this is no accident. I think she's been searching for Timber, and he's been dying without her. Sadly, I think we might be too late."

That's the last thing I heard him say before black took over my line of vision.

one of the better choices to come back. Then again, it's always entertaining when you hang out with vampires, am I right?"

He made a face. "Ridiculous creatures, I prefer my own blood."

"So I tell them. Every day." Alex winked. "And we're merely here as guides, with your awareness of course."

He looked around Alex toward me and then back. "Trying to change a past or a future?"

"Both." Alex's body pulsed with energy that hit me in waves of heat and longing. I gripped the reins I was surprised to find in my hand and kept watching. "Apparently you're about to make a deal with the devil and try to fix it in the worst way possible. I can't tell you what you will do, but I urge you to trust carefully."

Ra studied him and then stood to his twelve-foot height, placing both hands on Alex's shoulders. "I do not trust easily, not with the wars, not with the mortals pushing us from their realm. But I do trust a true son of the light even if he's part siren. So I will listen to your warning. Go with my peace. Furthermore, go with my permission in this time."

Alex bowed and then came back to us. I could tell something was wrong by his less confident swagger. When he was finally at my side, he looked up to Mason with fear in his eyes. "I improvised."

"What's that supposed to mean?" I hissed.

"It means," Alex whispered, "that we are smack dab in the middle of one of the greatest wars between the old gods that ever existed. The Great War. Most were banished. The Creator left them to their own devices. The original dark ones, more powerful than any, half human half god. They are the original creation. Like gods. The first of the last." Alex choked on the last part. "I'm an idiot, should have put two and two together, maybe my own sadness and arrogance didn't let me see what was right in front of me. You want a history lesson, look around you. These gods make us look like plastic toys. Their only weakness is they can't intervene with free will. Everything else is a free for all. And in our time, they are all but instinct."

"Except for you," I pointed out.

He glared. "I'm not allowed to go full god, one of the rules of actually enjoying my time on the immortal council. Last time didn't go so well." His eyes went dark as he shared a look with Tarek and Mason.

"I'm hungry." This from Tarek.

All of us gaped.

"What?" He shrugged. "Just because we're trying to undo something doesn't mean my appetite changes. And I can't survive off sand. I'm not Mason!"

"Thanks, man," Mason grunted.

"Up you go, princess." Before I could say anything Tarek had his hands around my waist and was lifting me up onto the horse attached to the other end of the reins I clutched. A lovely Arabian horse. *My* gorgeous Arabian horse.

Her coat was mostly white with faint shadings of gray at her feet. Her mane was braided and dyed different colors of blues and purples. She was so beautiful it hurt to look at her.

"Stop calling me princess." I grabbed the reins.

Whatever I said earned chuckles.

"What now?" I hissed as we turned in the opposite direction of Ra's temple.

"Thought your memory would be better now that we're here." Tarek shrugged. "Should we tell her?"

"No," Alex snapped. "It has to be natural, organic. She has to experience things the same and make a different choice than last time. Furthermore, so does he."

"Timber?"

Uneasiness fell over the three of them, but no one replied.

"Right?" I tried again.

"He's... not known as Timber here," was all Alex said.

"Who is he?" I almost didn't want to know.

"Death," Mason finally uttered as something flickered in his eyes, new knowledge maybe. "He is known as death."

CHAPTER SIXTEEN

TIMBER

Egypt, Valley of the gods

"Father wants a virgin." The first thing my brother Horus said as we rode through the valley, taking inventory of all the gods that no longer resided with us, and furthermore, taking a tally of the ones still living who could defy us taking over the gods of the Greeks.

Not many remaining.

Thank the Creator.

Dirty bastards anyway, less powerful, more whiny. Pity since they were beautiful to look at, horrible to escort to the Abyss, always arguing over why they should never die when that was the Creator's plan all along.

An end, so He could finally start over, a new beginning.

My horse neighed.

"Quiet, Styx," I murmured as we pulled to a stop in front of the Temple of Ra. It had been years since we'd visited. I was pulled to it now, and I couldn't explain why.

My own grandfather looked like my brother, but even he was withering with age; it showed in his laugh lines, I wondered when he would finally be done, finally want to be set free from the rules that bound us to this earth.

"Did you hear anything I just said?" Horus asked with a soft chuckle.

"Yes. A virgin. Good luck finding a goddess that will actually appease him." I snorted.

"He's already found one. A human," Horus said under his breath.

I turned and gave him a confused look. "What? A human?"

"Royal." He shrugged. "Like that helps."

"Exactly!" I was disgusted. "We don't mix for a reason. Our bloodlines don't allow it. The last time it happened, Ra was not pleased, the Creator was even more displeased, and we were almost at war!"

"Her father," Horus kept talking, "is one of the last remaining Greek gods with sustainable power, Apollo. The alliance would be beneficial to everyone involved."

"You said she was human," I corrected.

"She's mostly human, apparently Apollo wanted her to have a normal life, so he begged the Creator for a boon—take her godliness from her blood, but leave her beauty."

I snorted. "And he said yes?"

"He said there was a reason."

My body was on edge as I clenched my teeth. "There always is, isn't there?"

Horus nodded his head toward the temple. "We should visit."

"He'll burn us on site."

"Maybe you..." Horus said with a burst of laughter.

I just rolled my eyes. "It's not my fault he's scared of me now that he knows what I do. He will always fear his death. I don't take it personally."

"You shouldn't. Not until you surpass him in power, as you're already doing."

I ignored him, even though I knew there had been whispers that the more my father fed his dark side, the more strength the Creator gave me, the more dominion I had.

"We all see it," Horus said softly. "One day you will take over and I'm glad for it. No other god is better."

"You mean older," I joked trying to take the attention away from myself as much as possible, because if my own brother knew this, then everyone else did too, including my own very jealous father.

"Try not to break a hip," he teased.

We both laughed and then raced across the desert, back to our father's temple and his people.

It was a beautiful prison painted as one of the most enormous temples in the Nile.

Set wasn't evil, but he wasn't good either. He bargained, he wagered, he craved the war between the last remaining gods because he knew with his two sons on his side, along with Ra, we wouldn't fail.

The Greeks didn't stand a chance.

Which begged the question, why an alliance?

"Why," Horus said echoing my very thoughts as if they were his own. "Indeed."

Two hours later…

I could live a million years and never tire of the sight. The gates of Set and Osiris. White marble columns rose from the desert floor. Brilliant jewels shone from above, casting beams of colored light in all directions. Everywhere the eye could see, gleaming gold decorated pillars and trellises, and more jewels winked from settings in the marble walls. And no matter where we were inside the giant city gates, there was laughter, the smell of food, sweet meats, flowers. Every breath inhaled was a gift of fragrance from the most expensive perfume money could buy.

The white marble streets were lined with our people, happy, safe, protected from death, destruction—protected from me as long as they served the Creator.

It always amazed me how easily humans forgot the danger

that lurked in that temple, that skulked mere feet from where they stood—from where they refused to worship.

To worship me was forbidden as long as my father sat on the throne. I would forever walk among them, feeding off their fear as much as I would their worship. Then again, I didn't want it. Part of me knew the Creator was a jealous being. He didn't want humans worshipping his creation; he wanted them worshipping Him.

And I couldn't find it within me to argue such a valid point—my brother agreed with me at least on that front. It was like worshipping the meat once it was cooked rather than thanking the cow for existing in the first place and giving up its life.

Ridiculous.

We walked farther into the inner city while people watched in awe, many of them whispering, others hiding.

The main temple was said to be the tallest building on the planet, over seventy stories high with over a thousand rooms in the actual temple itself, not to mention the hordes of animals kept within its walls for food and entertainment.

The temple of Osiris looked like heaven on earth, the opposing temple the darker of the two—Set's faced the east to honor Ra with the sunrise, and at sunset it looked as though someone had dipped it in orange paint.

The only thing missing was the gate to Heaven, which had long since been destroyed. Once the Creator spread humans throughout the universe, it was dangerous, He had admitted, for them all to understand one another.

Our people had no idea that the gates they often walked by were actually the gates of Tartarus—Hell itself. Because my father was not a good man—well, he wasn't a man at all but either way goodness was not in his makeup—power hungry, jealous to his core.

His desire was always more.

His curse was to never be satisfied.

And it seemed to be getting worse with age. While his sons thrived, he plotted, and I feared the day he would one day push one or both of us too far.

I felt it in the air around me.

In the way, my skin prickled with awareness.

Rumors spread that he was the god of the demonic race, a way for the Creator to prove to the gods that there was a fate worse than death—being trapped as an immortal, cursed to live in a constant thirst with the need to feed on the very humans you swore to protect.

I gripped my throat. I was a god, but that baser instinct still ran through me, watching, waiting to attack. I knew the blood that ran through me, that if my soul was one day lost, that part of me would take over. It was the only way the Creator kept balance between the gods and their enormous amounts of freely given power, the very real threat that you could give in to darkness—and come out the loser, or that he could snap his fingers and everything would be lost.

I rebuked the darkness on a daily basis, however, because I was a god.

And not just any god.

I was the god of death.

The taker of souls.

I smirked as we made our way up the sleek marble stairs into the golden throne room.

Let them try to take me. I'd been missing a good fight.

CHAPTER SEVENTEEN

KYRA

I wasn't hiding my emotions very well, something that the guys commented on for the next hour as we traveled to the land of my apparent father. I wondered what he looked like. I wondered if he would give me the same look of disappointment and sadness my father back in my world did, every time I wasn't able to find what they were looking for.

Every time I failed.

I pressed a hand to my chest and gasped when I encountered it. "My necklace! I have my necklace!"

"Interesting that it would travel back with you—meaning it has already been given, possibly for protection," Alex said in a silky voice that immediately calmed my nerves, especially since I started to hear cheers as we moved our horses over the sandy hill.

The minute I reached the top, my jaw dropped.

Grecian style white pillars surrounded at least thirty square miles of jungle, right in the middle of the desert! A huge menacing white castle stood in the middle of the city, its walls so high it seemed impossible to penetrate. Ivy had wrapped itself around the structure, giving it a fairy tale look.

I tried to wipe the smile off my face—and failed. This wasn't exactly the adventure I had signed up for when I started working at Soul—I had this immediate need to show Timber, to tease him, get a rise out of the grumpy sarcastic demon whose kisses felt like a drug.

Mason grunted. "You're blushing."

I scowled in his direction. "I was just thinking."

"Penny for your thoughts," Tarek mused. "Oh wait, I think I know exactly what you were thinking about. Odd that a demon bite would feel so satisfying, am I right?"

I wanted to crawl under my horse and hide. All three of them snickered like they knew every gory detail. I held my head high. "It was fine."

"She's blushing harder," Tarek quipped. "Didn't know Timber had it in him. Isn't he missing his heart?"

"You'd think he would have asked for that instead of a used soul." Tarek sighed in amusement. "But no, now we have to do the heavy lifting."

I frowned. "Is he… I mean, he's going to be okay, right?"

"As long as you don't fail," Tarek said cheerfully then added, "No pressure. And you're going to find out very soon, because it looks like the solstice is starting, which means you're about an hour away from visiting the temples of Osiris and Set."

I frowned as we neared a creek that ran down the path leading into the city. Orange trees in full bloom surrounded us; it smelled like heaven!

"What do I do when I get there?"

Tarek stiffened. "Just be yourself."

"Anything else?"

Mason reached over and patted my hand. "Try not to faint."

That wasn't helpful.

"What about my father? And mother? Here in this time? Will they know?"

"Doubtful." Alex sounded confident. "You've been reborn, so you're still you replacing you in the past, the same way you've been doing it in the future. Timber, however, will not be the same as he's currently trapped in the present probably battling his own inner demons, if he's even awake."

Or still alive. He didn't say what we were all thinking.

He couldn't die.

I refused it.

The thought of it had me feeling so sick to my stomach I wanted to cry. It was weird how attached I suddenly felt.

The gates to the city opened, and we trotted the horses through. I tried to stay in between Tarek and Mason while Alex went ahead of us, looking every inch the god he was.

People cheered.

I could get used to this.

I smiled.

"Wave," Mason coughed under his breath.

I lifted my right arm and waved, and noticed that I had jewels covering every single finger, black rubies to be exact.

Was that why my hand felt heavy?

I suddenly wondered what I looked like.

Back home my hair was cropped and I had blue streaks, call it my version of rebellion, I liked cowboy boots and jean shorts and preferred tank tops and sweatshirts to anything fancy.

I looked down. I was in a white dress that wrapped tightly around my body, I was wearing thin gold sandals that wrapped all the way up to my thighs, I could tell because my dress has a slit on each side.

I stopped waving when the massive castle gates opened to us.

Why were we going to the castle?

Both men were silent as Alex gave a two-finger salute and led his horse ahead of us into the inner gates.

A trail of yellow and pink roses led up the stairs and toward a massive throne made of black stone.

And sitting there was a carbon copy of my father, only this man looked a lot more like Alex.

He had golden flaxen hair, his eyes were glowing gold, and his armor was swirled in red and silver.

He stood and spread his arms wide in a way my dad had never done before, in a way that made me feel like I belonged in the past more than I belonged in my present. Tears pricked my eyes as someone—maybe Tarek? Mason? It could have been anyone, really—helped me from my horse. I didn't walk up the stairs. I didn't even register that this man was anything other than what I'd wanted my entire life—the way I'd wanted my dad to look at me. I'd never realized what I'd been missing.

This. Was. Love.

Despite wearing sandals, I sprinted up those stairs, and then I launched myself into his arms, hoping, praying they would wrap around me the way I dreamed.

And when they did.

I let a tear slip.

"Kyra," he whispered in a way so reverent, so deep and true that I kept my arms wrapped around his neck even though his skin felt hot like the sun.

He said my name like he knew me.

He said my name like I was his.

Slowly, this god, my father, pulled back and cupped my face, his hands covered in jewels of green and silver. "I missed you."

I opened my mouth to speak. His accent was slight, mine would be nonexistent. I couldn't cover up my American heritage, so I said. "I missed you too."

His eyes flickered and then narrowed, he looked behind me at the three massive figures then back to me. "It seems…" He hesitated. "…that we have a lot to discuss."

Shit, did he know?

How?

"All right." I ducked my head but didn't miss how he wrapped a protective arm around me and led me away, snapping his fingers behind him as Alex, Mason, and Tarek followed.

We didn't have to go far before I saw my mom, she was walking toward us, her arms outstretched, and then something odd flickered in her gaze with my dad. Massive doors swung closed, leaving us in a large room filled with a feast fit for a king. A long wooden table stood in the center, with several soft purple chase lounges scattered around it.

"Leave us," Dad barked.

Every single guard left.

At least my guard stayed. I recognized the annoyance in my dad's gaze, though it was weird seeing him actually express anything other than disappointment.

"I think..." My dad sat at the head of the table. "You should start at the beginning..." His eyes fell to Alex as his voice lowered. "Or perhaps... the end."

I stiffened. Where had I gone wrong? He'd seen me a total of five minutes. Tarek reached for my hand and squeezed it then helped me sit down while Mason sat on the other side.

Both of them pulled off their helmets at the same time earning a gasp of horror from both my parents.

Well that didn't bode well for us.

"Watcher," Dad whispered his eyes locked on Mason. "How are you not chained to the Abyss!"

"Funny story." Alex flashed him a grin then pulled off his own golden helmet. His orange hair fell past his shoulders as his eyes blazed the same color in my dad's direction. "Okay I lied, maybe not funny... as much as, surprise?"

My mom covered her mouth with her hands and

whispered with trembling fingers. "We have failed. That is what you're telling us?"

I forgot how frail my mother looked. She was very human in appearance, with long jet-black hair, pale blue eyes, and golden-brown skin that made her even more flawless. She was wearing a white, floor length dress that wrapped around one shoulder and draped down to the floor. From the way it glinted in the light, I thought maybe it was dusted in diamonds.

"Not necessarily," Mason answered from my right. "We've been sent back to correct a wrong. One of our own—one of *your* own is dying and the only direction the archangel gave us was something even we can't warn you about."

My dad was quiet and then his eyes flashed blue. "How many years?"

I shifted in my seat while Alex answered.

"You really don't want to know that."

"Tell me!" Dad's voice boomed like thunder in that room.

I clutched Tarek's hand tighter. He wrapped a muscled arm around me, his eyes flashing a bright brown as a low growl rumbled in his chest.

Mom gave him a weary look. "They walk with the Kings of the earth."

"The King," Mason corrected, standing to his full height. "You're lucky I don't require a bow."

Oh, hell. My dad looked pissed but did nothing.

Mason joined Alex. "As far as how many years from this present date, it isn't for you to know. It changes nothing, it helps nobody. Just know that the gods of old are either imprisoned for intervening or they are…" He eyed Alex. "…

diminished in their powers so that they don't hurt the human race—or themselves for that manner. The Creator has given us all free will, and we choose to live amongst the mortals, meaning we choose to live with a diminished power."

"And the rest of the Watchers?" My father asked.

"The Creator—" Mason's voice caught and he swallowed hard. "Has set us all free."

My dad looked ready to pass out. "Impossible! What they did was unforgivable! They were given one job, to wa—"

"Blah blah blah, yes we know." Alex waved him off. "And they fell in love with humans and started a war, blah bloody blah. We've lived through these wars, no need to repeat a history lesson."

My dad's eyes met mine. "You would sacrifice the life you live now in order to change the course of your own history?"

I swallowed slowly. "No, I would sacrifice the life I have now in order to change the course of history."

"Who?" Dad leaned forward. "King Set? Is that who we are talking about? Your betrothed?"

I gaped. "B-betrothed?"

I was immediately transported to the dream of riding into the temple, seeing the massive castle and King Set on his throne.

"You are the Princess of Apollo, and you agreed to sign the betrothal covenant to align our two divided countries days ago. We ride in an hour." He stood. "I don't know how things are done in your time, but in ours we honor our promises to the death."

This was bad. So bad.

"But—"

"She's just nervous," Tarek interjected smoothly. "She of course has traveled back in time to save the one her soul craves. After all, isn't love worth the sacrifice?"

My dad visibly relaxed. "Yes, yes it is. I'm glad to hear it." He walked around the table and held out his hands to me.

I took them. They were warm, loving, and finally he cracked a smile. "I may be a god of this time, but I am still a father, I am still blood." He leaned down and pressed a kiss to my forehead. "Regardless of the timeline you are from, I have loved you for an eternity and will continue to do so. Promise me you will not fail, because I don't think I can bear it."

Pressure weighed against my chest as I nodded with confidence I didn't feel. "I will not fail."

"My little princess." He pulled me in for a hug just as my mom joined us, the three of us stood there, hugging, and warmth spread across my skin.

This was what I had been missing my entire life.

It was unfortunate, that I most likely sacrificed that very thing—to have it.

CHAPTER EIGHTEEN

TIMBER

Egypt, Same Day

I was in a foul mood as I paced restlessly in the palace. There were at least two people in Soul, my lesser temple, waiting for answers that they knew I couldn't give. It was always the same.

In minutes, I would be judging yet another human female, pure? It only mattered to my father because he was arrogant and wanted power. He wanted his people to know that he deserved a soul as pure as the light that held it.

As pure as Ra himself.

I rolled my eyes in disgust. How many years would this go on? This ridiculous power struggle, this war?

I moved into the light room. Humans were always shocked that my temple held more light than the rest—they misunderstood my darkness for evil when it was there for balance. Besides, souls glowed, something they didn't take into account when they entered and begged me to make sure they were given either a second chance or were sent to Heaven and not Tartarus.

I eyed the small golden scale next to my white throne. I had five minutes and sadly, that was all it would take.

Darkness swirled beneath my feet with each step I took toward my throne, when I sat, the first man approached. I was used to Pharaohs. This man was a farmer, his skin bronzed from the sun, his hands strong, bruised, callused.

I liked him immediately.

A rarity for me.

"Name?" I leaned back in my seat and reached for my goblet of wine.

"Perseus." His voice sounded as strong as his countenance.

"And to what do I owe the pleasure Perseus?"

He bowed low. "My dark prince, I only ask one thing."

"Only one? Must be my lucky day." I sighed. "Continue."

"My wife." His voice trembled. "She is heavy with child, and I fear—I fear she's too small to give birth, I ask that you don't make me choose between my love and my children if it comes to that. I ask that you take my soul to secure their lives. I'll serve an eternity in Tartarus, I'll—"

I held up my hand. He paled. "Do you think I'm in need of souls?"

He met my gaze, his brown eyes clear as day. "I think any god would be in need of good souls, loyal ones, ones who know exactly the bargain they make when they enter these walls."

A slow smile spread across my lips as I whispered, "Keep your soul, Perseus. If it is her time to die I cannot stop that, but—" I snapped my fingers as a shimmer of light appeared in front of my fingertips. "The essence of Ra is the essence of life itself, gifted from the Creator. While I may not intervene in this instance, I give you a gift. Take this," The air shimmered again and then the light turned into a bright orange vial. "Give it to your wife the day of her labor, not any sooner, it will not only ease her pain, but give her and your boys extra strength as they are welcomed into this world."

He gasped. "I never told you they were boys."

"How would you know for sure anyway?" I shrugged. "Two healthy boys," My eyes went bright gold as I saw his possible futures, something I could only do to pure human blood. "Give her the vial."

Perseus grabbed the vial and burst into tears. "Praise you, prince of—"

"Silence." My voice boomed. "You will praise the Creator—for I know my place. I was made by his hands, given life by his very breath. Save your praises for him."

"Praise be to the Creator," he whispered. "Praise be to

his intelligent design in you, Prince of Darkness, Anubis of Egypt, Keeper of Souls."

I flinched. He'd used my entire name, a rarity for a human to even know my ancient name.

Stunned, I watched him walk away. A shiver ran down my spine as Horus walked in and whistled. "It's time."

My bitter mood was back as I snapped my fingers and felt the warmth of the jackal's blood course through my veins. Shifting into my ceremonial state once more for a father I wanted nothing to do with—and a girl who I was about to damn for an eternity.

"Let's go." I barked.

Horus followed me, his fingers brushing my shoulder as he whispered, "It feels different to me this time too."

I ignored the way my heart skipped—the first time in centuries.

Just as I ignored the sharp intake of breath that escaped my lungs when the woman in question, Princess Kyra, rode into the temple on a white horse, her guard flanking each side, her head held high.

Her.

My blood pumped.

Her.

That one.

My soul rejoiced, beat against my chest in an attempt to break free, to celebrate with hers. It was rare for a god to find a match.

And I, Anubis, the Prince of Darkness had just found mine.

My father's betrothed.

CHAPTER NINETEEN

KYRA

Egypt, Same Day

My dreams didn't prepare me for the lavishness of the temple or the castle within its walls, for the rose petals that fell from a place in the sky that was impossible to see or the smell of ambrosia as its heady scent filled the thick, hot air.

I was dressed in a golden gown that draped over my horse nearly hitting his hooves, it was held together by a black diamond in the front like a cape, the rest was wrapped around me in tight layer after layer of what felt like silk, except the material breathed.

Slits went up both legs as I sat in the saddle, hitting me mid-thigh, and as we stopped in front of the marble steps to the throne where King Set waited, I had never been more petrified in my life.

How did I know what was right? What was wrong?

Beside me, Alex, Mason, and Tarek were quiet. My dad and mom were so tense it felt more like a funeral march than a wedding betrothal, and even then I was minutes away from hurling onto the pristine white stairs.

I looked over to Tarek.

His gold helmet was back on his head but he must have seen me from the corner of his eye, he gave me a confident nod just as massive hands wrapped around my waist and helped me off my horse.

It was him.

The Jackal.

I gaped as his fingers burned against my skin in such a delicious way that I wanted to lean into him. My body had forgotten this part, where my heart felt like it might burst out of my chest at the sight of him.

It wasn't fear.

It was like coming home.

I gave him a bright smile only making him stiffen more as a hand pressed against my chest and pulled something blue out an inch. It tickled against his fingers, its tentacles wrapped around his tanned thumb like it was afraid he was going to let go.

I had to stop myself from saying, *keep it, it's yours.*

When he pressed it back into my chest I felt such loss that my knees knocked together.

"Pure," his voice rasped. "Of both body and soul."

I remembered this entire thing differently.

This wasn't how it happened the first time.

Then again, I wasn't the same person was I?

Furthermore, neither was he.

I met his gaze. Even as part beast he was beautiful with a long sharp snout and matching pointy black ears. His chest heaved as he watched me. Something stirred inside as my fingers burned to reach out, to touch that jet-black fur.

"Well then," King Set laughed and spread his arms wide. "Bring my betrothed here."

My feet didn't budge.

He was massive, the King, at least twelve feet tall with jet black hair and eyes that glowed both red and gold switching every few seconds. They reminded me of Timber's eyes, and longing pulsed through my body.

I was doing this for him.

For Timber.

For the beast currently holding his hand out to me.

I took it because I had no other choice.

"Prince Anubis," Set said through clenched teeth. "You will escort the princess to the throne."

Anubis.

Anubis.

Of course he was.

The Prince of Darkness.

The damned.

My mythology or what I thought was mythology, was

rusty, but thanks to my parents I knew exactly what Anubis did. He judged the souls, determining where they would be placed in the afterlife.

He was also one of the oldest gods mentioned in mythology, some say more powerful than the one I was supposed to be marrying.

His head tilted toward me and with a slight growl he changed into a man, a beautiful man.

"Timber," I whispered.

It was Timber.

My heart hammered so loud against my chest I figured he was going to tell me to calm down.

Instead, he inspected me like I was a science experiment, his golden eyes narrowing into tiny slits as he held out his hand. "Princess."

Tears stung, but didn't fall.

I kept them in as his warmth wrapped around me, the simple graze of his hand was enough to make my knees buckle.

"Remember," I whispered under my breath. "I need you to remember."

He jerked his head toward me. "You dare speak to the god of death?"

I lifted my chin. "You dare look at the face of Apollo's one and only daughter?"

He stopped walking, his eyes searching mine.

"Anubis," Set was making his way toward us. "In this century, if you please."

Timber looked at his father and then to the left of the

throne where another godlike man stood, his face softened as they shared a look.

"Brother!" The man jogged ahead of Set, he was in front of us in a flash. "What the ever-loving hell is going on?" His voice was quiet, we had seconds before Set would be standing in front of us.

"I need some time alone with Ti—Anubis," I clarified "Before Set and I…" I moved my hands. I had no idea what happened next. Did Set just take me in front of a priest or was that not how gods did things? There had to be a ceremony of sorts. I just hoped it wasn't today.

Time, I needed more time.

"Set won't like it," Anubis said under his breath.

"Set can go to Hell," I muttered, earning a curse from both Horus and Anubis.

"You can't intervene." Horus nodded to Anubis. "Remember, brother, or everything will be for naught."

"Understood." Anubis sounded so cold, calculating, at least some things didn't change, right? Timber in my time was the same way, like he was constantly doing math in his head.

And then Set was there, stopped in front of me. I was maybe up to his waist. Power radiated from his black armor as he eyed me up and down. "Are you scared, daughter of Apollo?"

"No, King Set, why? Are you?"

Horus burst out laughing while Anubis seemed to go completely still.

The crowd watched in rapt fascination as I waited for Set

to either murder me or appreciate my sense of humor. They should have given me a damn manual!

I felt it then, the presence of Alex behind me, the sharp intake of breath around the crowd as Mason and Tarek moved to stand beside me, both of them without their helmets.

One looking every inch the fallen angel, the other a menacing watch dog, and I knew without looking that Alex had gone full god.

Perfect.

We were going to die, weren't we?

Set took a step back his eyes wide. "What's the meaning of this?" He glared at my father. "You dare bring a fallen into my temple?"

"I prefer king," Mason said in a bored tone. "You can thank me later for the very ground beneath your feet."

Alex's warm chuckle wasn't helpful as he put a hand on Mason's shoulder and shrugged. "You'll have to forgive him, he's still part wolf, forgets his place, just like you have, my king. After all, is it not proper to bow to royalty? Kyra's godlike essence may have been taken from her blood, but she is still a princess and soon to be your queen, am I right?"

Oh, hell.

Set's jaw snapped closed as he very slowly inclined his head. I was pretty sure that was all I was going to get.

Too much testosterone swirled between all the men.

I was afraid someone was going to pull a weapon so I did the only thing I could think to do.

"Should we go inside the temple? And make a toast to King Set?" *When all else fails, build their ego.* Hadn't my dad told me that the gods liked to talk about themselves? About their own prowess? Power?

Set seemed to soften in that moment as he gave me a bright smile that I'm sure any woman would love to have directed at her, but beneath it was something more sinister, like I wasn't going to be marrying him, but sacrificed on an altar so he could keep his beauty, his power.

"Of course." Set nodded. "You may bring your... protectors, though I should warn you... the last god who challenged me was sent immediately to Tartarus, compliments of my son Anubis. We don't take kindly to threats. Death would be better than facing Anubis while he draws your soul from your body before sending you into eternal darkness."

I could have sworn I heard Alex whisper under his breath, "Cool story, bro."

"They'll behave," I said quickly.

"Never thought I'd see the day when a human has immortals on a leash like a pet." Set's mocking laugh had me digging my nails into the palm of my hand as he gave us his back and started walking back up the marble stairs.

Servants moved around us in a flutter of black and red. The men were shirtless, wearing only black loose pants, and the women were in dark red dresses that were tied at the waist and strapless; so much material had to be heavy.

"Why red and black?" I wondered out loud.

It was Timber, or Anubis, who answered. "Red is the color of the blood that has been spilled for the humans to live in this world with free will."

I nodded. "And black?"

"A reminder, of what humans' future holds—when I take their souls."

My eyes widened. "Do you carry all the souls?"

"Yes." He rolled his eyes. "In my pocket, care to see?"

I grinned. "Sarcasm, how surprising."

He jerked his head down to me. "You play a dangerous game, princess."

"Afraid you're going to lose?"

He shook his head. "Exactly the opposite. I'm afraid I'll win."

With that he moved ahead to join his father, leaving Horus by my side with the guys on the other.

"Forgive him." Horus had bright blond hair and blue eyes that seemed to flicker with the same gold as Timber's. "There is a lot that weighs upon his mind."

"Like what?" I asked as casual as I could as we made our way into a large room with several tables of food and what looked like wine.

"Careful," Horus said in a sing-song voice. "You cannot trick a god."

"What's that supposed to mean?" I asked.

His eyes flashed gold. "Maybe you should have asked your parents that question before standing in front of our father. They should have coached you better."

My skin broke out into goose bumps. "Coached?" That word didn't exist in this time, I knew that much.

"Isn't that the correct word?" Horus asked. "You are not in your time, Kyra. You're lucky that Anubis's darkness has shielded you from our father. Pray he never finds out that you've traveled back."

"Because he'll kill me?"

"No." His eyes flashed again. "Because he'll suddenly remember that the gods can move through time—and he'll leave this world for yours."

Well, shit. "Can you?" I asked "Move through time?"

"I choose to limit myself as does my brother. The gods belong here, there is no place for us in the future. You've seen your protector in your time. The Creator would not allow us to rule there the way we do here, but that wouldn't stop Set from trying."

Horus pulled out a chair for me, it was purple velvet, and so soft I let out a sigh as I settled in it and then asked, "Why would he try?"

"Because his power is dwindling. It's why he needs you."

"Oh." My eyes flickered to Set as he discussed something with Anubis and then pointed at me, his smile cruel. "Why is it dwindling?"

"You ask a lot of questions." He sighed like he was annoyed but he seemed to be enjoying our conversation enough to sit across from me and smile.

I shrugged. "Like you said I'm out of time, I'm curious."

"Humans are so convinced that anything which is light is pure and good whereas darkness is evil. What if it was the exact opposite? The absence of light is not evil, the mind is evil. It is where we make decisions that alter the course of history. Anubis is one of the purest gods in existence, his darkness protects, it heals, it kills, it gives life. His very existence helps keep the balance between immortals and humans. It bothers my father, has created a jealousy that runs so deep that it has caused a cancer in his soul. A sick soul starts to fester, especially with a god. The baser instincts start to take over. In my father's instance, and in ours, we turn into something else entirely, a reminder to stay pure, a reminder of who created us in the first place."

This. This was it. This is what happened to Timber! "So…" I was desperate for more information. Alex, Mason and Tarek had even leaned in. "Out of curiosity, if one of you loses your soul… or if one of you is… cursed, what happens?"

Horus narrowed his eyes. "Is that why you're here, human?"

"Maybe." I gulped. "Maybe not."

He sighed. "Only Anubis can pull a soul from a body."

"Oh." Deflated I sat back against the chair.

"Set traps them."

"What?" I nearly collided with Mason who had suddenly jerked to his feet at the same time.

He ignored me and whispered. "And I, Horus Prince of Light, can set them free."

CHAPTER TWENTY

TIMBER

Egypt, Same Day

"Something's not right." My father paced in front of me. His smile was in place, but I could feel the irritation burning on his skin, pulsing through the air. "Are you sure her soul is pure?"

Paranoid. He was being paranoid, another sign that he was losing his grip on his godhood.

One day, he would wake up and find horns.

I looked forward to that day more than I should.

"She's pure." I swallowed the bile in my throat. There was only one reason he would be so obsessed with the purity of her heart and soul—the purity of her body.

He was going to marry her.

And then he was going to suck her soul dry.

I narrowed my eyes at him. "How long have you been planning this?"

He jerked his head in my direction, and his skin took on an ash tone. "What?"

"She has the blood of Apollo running through her veins, the soul of a god and lucky for you it lacks the essence meaning she's no longer immortal. How. Long?"

A shaking hand reached for a goblet of wine. He downed it in one gulp and looked away. "I'm losing my power."

"Then pray to the Creator for more."

He snorted. "The Creator has abandoned us. Cursed us to the land of the humans. We do not die, we just lose our power more and more every year until we turn into—"

"Don't say it." I hissed

There weren't many of them, the demons that sucked on human souls, just old gods that had lost their way, a creation that was born out of necessity to stay in our godlike state.

Because the only way to stay powerful was to be remembered.

And people were forgetting.

We didn't need their worship to stay powerful. We just needed to be needed and as the gods stopped being needed, they started looking inward, getting paranoid, selfish, giving in to their baser desires, just making it worse as their power slowly gave way to the darkness that ran in all of our veins.

Born as gods, not made.

First of the last.

Last of the first to be reborn into the baser race of demons.

I shook my head and stared at my father. "What did you say?"

He shrugged. "Nothing."

I looked over my shoulder. As long as I didn't touch her, I would be okay. As long as she didn't look at me like she loved me. As long as I didn't have to touch her soul again, to feel the way it tried to wrap itself around my skin... I would be fine.

Her only solace would be the simple fact that I, Anubis, would escort her body after my own father took the one thing he needed to stay powerful.

I could already hear her screams.

I would do that, to my other half.

To my mate.

For what?

To give my father more power he didn't need?

"She wants to speak with you." Horus slapped me on the back. "Something about needing time before the ceremony."

A ceremony I was supposed to perform.

Fantastic.

I turned to my father. He seemed annoyed. But when wasn't he annoyed? He flicked his hand in her direction. "She has twenty-four hours."

Hell.

I nodded and then slowly made my way over to Kyra. Her

protectors were circled around her, touching her, laughing with her as if we weren't within the temple walls.

As if this wasn't sacred.

Dangerous.

I knew her mother and father would have already been led to their rooms while they waited for the marriage.

And I hated that I wanted to tell Apollo to run and never come back, take his daughter with him, and beg Ra for protection.

Trapped. All of us.

"Kyra," I rasped. Her name felt like honey on my tongue. "You have twenty-four hours before my father makes you his." The words burned my mouth. "Is there anything else you need?"

She stood and held out a shaking hand. "I need to be alone. With you."

My knees almost buckled as I stared at that small hand.

So innocent.

Did she know what she was asking?

That gods were never alone with women.

It wasn't done.

Not in a million years would it ever be done.

Until now.

The man with the orange hair stood, his eyes blazed. "Anubis, you will want to speak with her alone, trust me."

"My father won't like it," I said through clenched teeth.

"Oh, that." He shrugged. "I'm part siren. I'm a fantastic distraction for males, females, plants," He started counting off on his fingers

The Watcher chuckled. "He's not wrong, though I wish he were."

"Tell me about it." The wolf winked at me.

Who were these people? And why did they feel so familiar?

The wolf chose that moment to grin and nod his head. "Soon, my man, very, very soon, just be careful."

"Mind reader?" I guessed.

"Sort of." He just shrugged. "Trust me, you'll want to hear what she has to say, and can it please be fast?" He looked around. "The longer we stay…"

"Stay?" I repeated. "You're leaving?"

"It's complicated," Kyra offered and then waved her hand in front of me again. "Shall we?"

"One rule." I eyed her hand. "You can't touch me."

Her adorable nose scrunched up. "Why?"

"Because…" I sighed. "It hurts."

"Your skin?"

"My heart," I whispered and gave her my back. "This way."

Her shocked expression didn't help the way my blood was roaring through my system as I took her as far away from Set as possible.

The Gardens.

I wasn't sure why I led her there, but it seemed right, to bring her around as much life as physically possible so she forgot that she was speaking to death itself.

I wanted to ask the Creator why.

Why now?

Why give me the one thing I couldn't have?

It wasn't fair.

I felt like I was in a game of Senet I could never win. Was doomed to lose before I even began.

We walked in silence down the stone paths and into the rose garden. The perfume of the flowers was dense, cloying, almost too much to handle as I led her toward the farthest stone wall, with its fountain and swimming pond. The water was so clear you could see all the way to the bottom. People used to believe that it was the fountain of youth.

Until they drank of it and realized it was just very cold, beautiful water.

"Wow." She grinned up at me with reckless abandon. I was so dumbstruck, so confused that I forgot to even respond to her, just stared her down in awe. "It's beautiful! How did you know I loved roses?"

"I didn't." I found my voice. "But to be fair, who hates them?"

Her smile was addicting, just like her voice. She tucked her dark hair behind her ears and shrugged. "Lots of people fail to appreciate the beauty of this world."

"You're not one of those people."

"No." She spread her arms wide and did a little twirl then faced me. "You're beautiful too. Angry, but beautiful."

"I'm not angry," I snapped.

Her eyebrows rose as if to challenge me.

I sighed. "I'm not. Angry that is. I'm just cautious."

"Hmmm." She seemed to find that interesting. And I found the way she reacted to everything fascinating. I reached out to touch her then jerked my hand back.

What the hell was I doing?

"Saw that," she said without looking up at me. "So I have

something to tell you, and I'm not sure how you're going to take it so I'm just going to say it, all right?"

I frowned. "All right…" Even then, my skin buzzed with the need to touch hers, to hold her in that place, against my chest.

I would have fallen in love with every hair on her head if she let me, with every inch of that body, with every flaw, every success. I would have loved her until my life was over.

My soul knew she was mine.

And I wanted so badly to take.

I focused on the smell of roses, on her inquisitive green eyes, on the way that she playfully bounced from one foot to the other without realizing it.

On the smell of cinnamon as she moved the air between us.

"Okay," She took a deep breath. "Like a Band-Aid. Just rip it off."

I smirked. "Is that what you meant to tell me? What's a… band… aid?"

She waved her hand in front of me, "Never mind, look, I'm not Kyra. I mean I am Kyra and I'm here as Kyra, shit this isn't going well," I laughed at her curse, wishing all human women were this adorable, and then realizing it would be death to us if they were. "So, okay, my boss…" She winced. "My friend, the person that…" She frowned. "He's a demon."

"Demon," I repeated, looking around. "A demon is your friend."

"Right." She licked her lips, I was momentarily distracted by her pink tongue, my focus was horrible, wasn't it? "He was cursed. He keeps saying he's the last of the first or the first of the last."

I stiffened immediately. I knew what that meant... did she?

"Anyway, he's dying. He has this tattoo in the middle of his hand. It has an eye and then branches."

My entire body went still. This was bad, very bad. This meant my father had done the unthinkable. He'd trapped the soul of a god, sending it into hibernation. But why?

"The branches are taking over." She kept talking. "He passed out, and we were sent to fix what he did wrong, to fix..." Her eyes locked on mine. "...what *you* did wrong."

I jerked my head in her direction. "What I did wrong?"

"You." Her eyes welled with tears. "I'm trying to save you."

"I'm right here." I panicked at the sight of her sadness. Was she losing her mind?

"No, the *you* in the future. You're a Demon King. You look almost identical save the height, and you said you borrowed a soul to feel, and you kept saying I needed to remember, that we needed to remember, so an angel sent us back. We just have to make a different choice about... something, and you'll be fine, I think."

I stared her down, my entire body was heavy, because I knew, in that moment, that no matter what she said to me, this woman, I would eventually take her, maybe not today, maybe not tomorrow, but I would take her before he killed her, before he sucked her dry.

I would claim her.

I would make that sacrifice.

I stumbled backward. "You."

"Me." She bit down on her lip. "I want to save your life, Anubis."

"It's too late," I whispered. "Because of you, I'm already dead."

CHAPTER
TWENTY-ONE

KYRA

Egypt, Same Day

I flinched from his words. It felt as if he'd slapped me. "I'm here so you don't die, not because you're already dead."

He shook his head. "You don't know of what you speak."

Okay, so now he was making me want to punch him. I pressed my hands against his chest, earning a growl from his lips as he gripped my wrists almost painfully. "Then tell me, because I'm risking everything in being here."

"Do you love me?" he whispered. "Is that why you're here?"

"I don't know." Tears filled my eyes. "I just know I don't want to live without you, I want you to live!"

His gaze softened. "You don't understand."

"Then make me!"

"This." He gripped my wrists tighter. "This pulse between us, this push, this pull, we fit." His eyes flashed gold. "You are mine, daughter of Apollo. Don't you realize? You are my half. My soul recognizes you and only you. So if I did something wrong, it was in choosing you over my father, choosing you over my blood. I can't do it again."

My body swayed toward him, needing more, more skin, more of his voice, more of everything. I saw us then, holding hands, laughing, memories of stolen kisses in the great hall, of discussing children, a future.

He didn't release me, just stared into my eyes as this movie of our lives played while we watched.

"I'll love you forever. It doesn't matter. The worst he can do is curse me, but I'll find you, Kyra, I'll find you anywhere!" he pledged.

"I know." Tears filled my eyes. "I'm yours."

"You are mine." He swore against my mouth, touching my belly. "And soon we'll have a family, we'll leave, I'll speak to him."

Our lives flashed forward.

"Sixty days." Timber kissed my head. "Sixty days until the curse is upon us."

I wrapped my arms around his body. "Was sixty days together, worth his wrath?"

"Yes," he said. "Worth it to make you my wife, worth it to know that one day we will find each other again."

Memories charged forward. Ra stood in front of us. "I can't counter what has been done. You made your choices, both of you, choosing each other, going against Set, against the rules of intervention. You will be punished, your souls will be lost, but," He held up his hand. "The Creator has agreed with my pleas, and one day, they will find each other. One day."

Anubis nodded. "It is enough."

I gripped his hand. "It's enough."

I slid my hands up his chest as he looked down at me, adoration in his gold eyes. The smell of roses fueled the hysteria, the need to touch him more.

And then his mouth was on mine.

We fell, in that moment, in the garden.

We fell together.

We made the same choice again.

Because the one thing I wasn't warned—your soul can't deny its other half, your heart can't lie.

And love—transpires through time.

No matter the cost.

Timber picked me up into his arms and twirled me around, pressing my body up against the rock wall as his hands moved to the black diamond holding my dress together. It pooled at my feet in an instant.

His hands moved across my naked skin as he ducked his head and kissed me again, his mouth was warm, and it tasted like a fall day. His tongue was so smooth as it traced the outline of my mouth.

This. I would die for this.

I would kill for this.

For him.

He growled. "He can't have you."

"Not when I have you," I answered. Wrapping my arms around his massive neck, he pressed light kisses to my lips only to deepen them as I moved my body against his. "I can't stop."

"That's the thing, Kyra," His lips moved against mine. "When you find that person, when you hold that gift, you're not supposed to stop. It's supposed to be effortless, perfect."

"Your father." I whimpered as Timber cupped my breasts like he was weighing them with the same hands he used to weigh souls. "He'll curse us again."

"And it would be worth it." His hands left, I hated the loss I felt. "Again."

"No." Tears filled my line of vision. "Not like this. I'm supposed to save you!"

His eyes were sad as he tilted my chin with this thumb. "I got to kiss you, I got to hold you—consider me saved."

"Anubis." I tested his name on my tongue, only to have him growl against my mouth again, kiss after kiss. I accepted, I gave in, because I found home in his arms, I found my very existence in those kisses.

Years I had searched for this.

And now I had it.

"Wait." I gently shoved him away. "We can't, you know we can't, we have to find a way to fix the future, not damn it again."

His chest heaved with exertion. "I won't lose you."

"You won't!" I was naked against his chest, could feel the warmth of his skin, count the beats of his heart. "The tattoo in the future, why would that happen?"

He sighed and ran a hand through his thick long hair. "Moving under the assumption that I took you for myself and left my father's house, that would mean I intervened, which we aren't allowed to do. It would mean my godhead would be shed and my soul would be up for grabs. It would mean giving in to the darkness that warred with the good. And if the tattoo is that of a seed it means that I borrowed a soul so I could feel again, because the one I had was most likely dormant or trapped."

My head jerked up. "Horus."

"Anubis, but thanks." He smirked.

"No, your brother! Horus! That's his thing right? Setting souls free?"

He narrowed his eyes. "Yes, but he can't go with you."

"Why?"

"Because..." Anubis sighed. "He would not be able to come back."

"Why?" I wanted to stomp my foot.

Timber cupped my chin. "Because it would mean he no longer existed in this timeline. He would be stuck in yours."

I nodded. "But to save you... would he do it?"

"Yes." A voice sounded behind Timber. He quickly covered me with his body. "When you didn't return, I got worried. Good to know her dress is already on the grass, brother." Horus gave him a sad smile. "I heard enough to know what this will cost me. Brother, know that there is nothing I will not do for you. I cannot imagine what the old Horus would have said."

Timber sighed. "He would have warned me of what would happen. He would have helped curse me in order to try to save me."

"Yes, probably."

"Why the change of heart?" Timber asked the same question I was going to.

"Because…" Horus's eyes danced between me and Timber. "I'm so damn tired of this existence. Maybe in the future I'll find happiness because there sure as hell isn't any here."

"You'll be limited," Timber pointed out.

"I'll be more normal after hundreds of years of being superior. I think I'll make it." Horus winked at me. "Let's grab your protectors before it's too late, and for the love of the Creator help her get her dress back on."

We moved quickly. I frowned. Did my dress look different? Yes… but why?

"Hurry," urged Horus.

He was right. There was no time to contemplate the meaning of the change. Timber and Horus walked ahead of me, back into the temple where it looked like Alex was the prime entertainment.

Set was drunk on something; whether it was wine or whatever story Alex was telling, it was working.

"What now?" I whispered, mainly to myself.

"I'll take care of it," Timber said gruffly. Leaving us, he approached his father and tapped him quickly on the chest, Sure enough a blue soul was pulled halfway out. Part of it was black with holes and a slime that looked like it was spreading, infecting the rest of it.

Is that what Timber meant when he said, the baser gods let their other instincts take over?

"Anubis!" Set's voice boomed. "What are you doing?"

"Saving her," Timber rasped, pulling his hand away and leaving the soul half hanging from Set's body.

"That won't last long," Tarek pointed out. "The soul will default back into his body."

"You need minutes." Anubis nodded toward us. "Go."

"Wait." I grabbed his hand. "What do you mean go? You're coming, aren't you?"

His smile was sad. "I exist already in that time, so no, I need to stay."

Tears stung my eyes. "I'm not leaving you!"

"Yes." Timber pressed a kiss to my forehead. "You are."

"But—"

"Thank you," his voice boomed, "For showing me even for a few minutes, what it feels like to be whole." He turned his back on me. "Now go."

"But—"

Tarek grabbed me by the arm, Horus grabbed the other, and then we were running down the palace stairs and jumping onto soldiers' horses—ones who were conveniently on the ground with blood spewing from their mouths.

Horus got on mine with me and kicked his heels into the mare's belly. We took off so fast I nearly fell off.

"Sorry." He gritted his teeth. "We don't have much time."

"How do we get back?"

"Pray," he shouted over the thundering hooves.

"What?"

"You heard me." He hit the reins harder as the horses galloped outside the city walls. "You must pray."

"And say what?" Was he insane?

"Ask to return to your time, to right a wrong, pray to the Creator. He has long since forgotten the sound of my voice."

"But you're a god.

"Still a creation," he pointed out. "Hurry. Even now I can feel my father stir."

"Okay." Tears ran down my cheeks as the sand-filled wind whipped against my face. "Please, take us home, take us back, so Horus can save Timber, so we can right this wrong…" Panic hit me in the chest as the horse tripped. "Please, Creator, please!"

What was I even doing?

The sun was ahead, it was hot against my skin, too hot. I blinked slowly as it started to set and then like a final bow, it winked—everything went immediately dark, cold.

I woke up with a start and stared into Cassius's sad eyes. They had turned completely white, and the room was chilled, frost clung to his face.

I was afraid to ask, but I had to. "Is Timber okay?"

"He's improving… slightly." Cassius looked down at the couch, and I followed his gaze.

Timber lay there, very still. His color was back, but the tattoo remained.

Trapped. My heart sank. He was still trapped. Even though I'd made a different choice.

Tarek, Alex, and Mason appeared to my left.

And then finally, Horus, looking every inch the god as he stared down at his brother and shook his head. "You idiot."

Cassius's eyebrows shot up, his gaze was deadly. "And who are you?"

"Horus, Prince of Light, and your only chance at saving that demon and restoring him."

"He's been restored, his soul that is." Cassius pointed out.

"That's the problem." Horus moved to the couch and pressed a hand to Timber's head. "You restored the cursed soul of a god. What did you think was going to happen? It's been trying to break free, but it's warring with the borrowed soul—the borrowed soul will continue to suck the life from the original until nothing is left but darkness—nothing is left but his demonic self."

"Who is he again?" Ethan walked in and gave Horus a once over. "Is there a costume party nobody told me about?"

Horus let out a growl. "Careful, vampire, my bark is worse than your bite."

I'd never seen Ethan react so violently as his fangs descended, eyes turning a bright shade of green.

"Horus!" My voice cracked. "Please, you have to help him."

Horus nodded. "I'm going to try." He pressed a massive hand to Timber's chest. "Remember, brother, remember what you are—who you are, remember your calling." He pressed both hands down. "I rebuke the borrowed soul in the name of the Creator. Be free!"

The house started to shake as the black tattoo slithered along Timber's pale skin as if something from the inside was trying to come out.

"You can't have him," a female voice rasped.

Horus stiffened. "Neither can you."

I looked around for the voice but saw nothing. The temperature in the room dropped as Cassius's wings spread out, ready to fight, ready to impale whatever came at us.

"Fight it." Horus encouraged his hand still on Timber's chest. "You must choose. Don't be like our father. Don't let a sick soul take everything from you. Remember who you are, Prince of Darkness, Anubis, Keeper of Souls!"

Timber's eyes burst open. They were pure gold, they were bright, and they were trained directly on me.

"Timber." I reached for his hand and squeezed. "Anubis..."

With a roar, something black wrapped around Horus's hand as he slowly pulled the darkness from Timber's body, the soul had flecks of blue still on it, but the rest of it looked like it was rotting.

Horus jerked the rest of it free and held it out to Cassius. "Destroy it."

Cassius took the black soul and crushed it with one hand. Black icicles fell to the ground and disappeared into thin air.

Timber moaned as gold pulsed across his skin, right before my eyes I saw him become restored to the man I had kissed only minutes previous, the man who I saw in my dreams, the one who said he was my other half.

The love of my life.

My soulmate.

The Prince of Darkness.

Timber's body convulsed and then as if jerking awake from a long night's sleep, he blinked and sat up, his eyes locked on Horus first. "Brother? What the hell are you doing here?"

"Good to see you too. Missed you. It's been what? A few thousand years? And thanks for saving my life, oh you're welcome Anubis, all in a day's work, also I'm trapped here now…"

"He's never had good manners." This from Alex who shot Timber an amused grin before winking over at me.

Nerves took over.

Would he remember past me and present me?

If we kissed in the garden was it in his memories now?

I had so many questions.

First and foremost, I just wanted to touch him, to feel his skin, to tell him… what? That I was in love with him? That I'd been in love with him for as long as I could remember? Only that I wasn't a god so my memories were still somewhat fuzzy? How did one even begin that conversation?

"Stuck," Timber repeated in a voice that was just slightly richer than before. "You're stuck in this time?"

"Apparently." Horus stood and then looked down at his clothes. "I imagine this would land me somewhere unpleasant?"

Mason winced. "You look like you belong at the Halloween store."

"What's Halloween?" Horus asked with genuine curiosity.

Alex laughed. "Ethan, show some fang. That right there, people really love vampires, they dress up as them. Ethan loves it, don't you, boy?"

Ethan flipped him off and then gave Horus a helpless look. "This is going to be difficult for you."

He shrugged. "I'm a god, I think I have it handled."

"Limited," Cassius pointed out. "And…" He stopped talking and then shared a look with Mason, who seemed to be in his own trance. "I think we should leave Kyra and Timber alone for a bit."

Alex kicked the chair. "Can't I just stay in the other room?"

Mason glared. "The last thing you need is to be around people who are going to be having all the…" He gulped. "Er, pinecones."

"What fresh hell kind of time is this?" Horus grumbled under his breath.

Timber was still silent, staring at me, his chest heaving.

His blond hair was as short as it was before, but his eyes had changed to pure gold as he watched me, his skin seemed to have this pulsing awareness beneath the surface. I couldn't tell if he was taller; he'd already been tall. He was still Timber, though he looked… content, whereas before he had seemed like he was constantly searching, grumbling, fighting.

"Time—" Cassius ushered everyone out. "—is a very fickle thing when you can exist outside of it." He shared a look with Timber. "We've just altered it. Be watchful."

The rest of the group followed him out of the house—Timber's house, and still I stared at him, waiting for him to say something.

Finally, I sat down on the couch next to him and shrugged. "Do I call you Anubis or Timber?"

"Call me Prince of Darkness." He said it with such a straight face that my jaw dropped. Had he had a personality transplant too? Was he going to be arrogant?

"I, uh…" I tucked my hair behind my ear at about the

same time he burst out laughing. I glared and then threw a pillow at him.

Of course he caught it with one hand and placed it on the floor beside him. Then he whispered. "I remember a garden… and a beautiful woman saying she would save me, that this time she would save me."

I sucked in a sharp breath. "What happened after we left?"

He shook his head. "I remember fragments, my father raging, and that's it, I'm sure it will come back to me, imagine a computer downloading thousands of years' worth of memories that have been suppressed."

"Oh." I nodded. "That makes sense." I stood and wrapped my arms around myself. "So you don't remember much of… us?"

He stood, towering over me as he reached for my arm and jerked me against his massive chest. "The memories that are the most clear—all have to do with a certain Princess of Apollo. You, and only you, have the power to bring me to my knees."

His kiss was soft.

I clung to his shirt and moaned into his mouth at about the same time he lifted me into the air and started walking. I broke the kiss. "Where are we going?"

"Making up for lost time," he said gruffly walking into his master bedroom and slamming the door behind him.

CHAPTER TWENTY-TWO

TIMBER

I remembered everything—mainly, I remembered her. Choosing Kyra despite my brother's protests, claiming her as my own before my father could get the chance, and being punished for our love.

We were given sixty days before my soul would be lost to hers, before the curse of the gods took over and completely obliterated me from the inside out.

I kissed her soundly again. The only problem with my memories was that I wished she was sharing them, but she had no idea. She had been reborn—she wasn't a god; she didn't know, and I did.

My love was all consuming.

My obsession bordering on dangerous.

And yet this human still looked at me like a science project, a pretty one she wasn't sure how to experiment with.

I'd never in my life had to woo a woman.

And now that I finally had her, the one that I'd searched for, the one who had saved me and risked her life to do it—I would need to woo her again so she understood.

We were made for one another.

There was no coming back from this.

I cupped Kyra's face. "I want you."

Her eyes locked on mine with uncertainty. "I want you too, I just feel like I'm missing some giant piece of our story."

"Let's make a new story," I rasped. "One in this time, together."

A small smile formed across her lips "You mean one where I'm the bartender and you're the cranky boss?"

"You'd be cranky too if you couldn't feel, yet remembered what it was like to feel everything, to be less powerful but not know why."

One of her dainty hands slid up my cheek. Her fingertips were like velvet. "Do you remember? Why you did it? Why you tried to borrow a soul?"

A weight settled against my chest. "The truth?"

"Please."

"I thought I was stronger. I thought without my soul I would be the same. But instead, nothing satisfied me. The only way to find satisfaction was to devour human flesh and even then I was always empty, but I had flickers of a past life where I'd been powerful—full. So I went to the only person who could give me what I craved. By then I was already lost to what I used to be, completely sick but unable to die. I barely lasted a hundred years without you in my life. When the goddess offered an exchange, I knew exactly what I was doing, but if it meant one day I would feel again, it would be worth it. So I allowed her to give me a borrowed soul, not knowing that mine would be restored thousands of years later. She was the goddess of death, you know her as, Mania, one of the Roman goddesses. She takes on different forms, different faces, and since the gods were all but extinct, I knew she would give me what I wanted."

Kyra sighed. "I'm sorry."

"Don't be." I wrapped my arms around her body and pulled her close. "It could have been worse."

She frowned. "I don't see how?"

"I could have lost you."

Her eyes flickered to my mouth. "You didn't, I just wish…"

"What?"

"I wish that I remembered more… of us."

"I know." I felt helpless, something I was hoping would be a rarity. Then again, I did have power, right? I would be limited, but maybe I could show her, maybe I had enough power to show her a glimpse. "I'm going to try something."

"Okay." She looked petrified.

I grinned. "It won't hurt. It's not like I'm biting you again."

She gulped. "Yes. That."

"You liked it."

"Maybe." She narrowed her eyes.

"Don't worry, I liked it enough for both of us," I whispered, lowering my head to hers, I pressed a kiss to her parted lips then deepened it as I placed my right hand on her chest. She jumped and then relaxed as power surged through my fingertips.

I felt her soul.

Felt the stirring.

I turned my fingertips, drawing her soul from her body. It clung to my hand just like I remembered, wrapped its tentacles around my fingertips so tight that I winced.

"It's your turn," I said against her mouth. "To remember."

I kissed her harder then, sliding my tongue into her mouth while holding her soul in the palm of my hand, letting it take whatever energy or memories it needed.

Kyra gasped and pulled away. "We were in the Great Hall."

"Yes." I felt my eyes flash with the memory, and my body burn.

"You, you tried to turn away and I..." She looked horrified. "I seduced you!"

"I was gladly seduced."

"You tried so hard to do the right thing." Tears filled her eyes. "And I just ignored it!"

"I told you not to touch me." I kissed her again, tasted her. "It hurt my heart, it made my soul shake in my chest—and then you did. I was brought down by one touch, to my very knees."

She trembled in my arms. "I was selfish."

"You were terrified," I corrected her. "My father was going to murder you."

Kyra shook her head. "No we were going to get married and…"

"Murder. You still had the soul of a goddess thanks to your father. Trust me when I say he was going to use you to buy himself more time… innocent of body and soul."

Kyra gasped. "And my parents knew?"

"How could they? They were blinded by the thought of peace."

I released her soul and waited while she stumbled back and sat on the edge of the bed, my bed.

It was like existing in two times, I was remembering everything but at the same time was still Timber, still my *old* self.

The only difference was the power I felt surging through my veins and the very real need I had to strip Kyra naked and keep her that way for the next decade.

I assumed it would be easy to get her to see.

Instead, in perfect Timber ridiculousness, I'd made it worse.

Once a demon always a demon, lucky me.

"I um…" She looked up, and I knew, this was what rejection felt like, when all you wanted was the person looking at you with regret and pity in their eyes knowing you would sell your soul for just one taste—and do it again and again until you were sick with it. "This is a lot right now."

I clenched my teeth, took a deep breath. "You should sleep."

"But this is your—"

"Don't argue with the cranky boss, Kyra." I smiled sadly. "I'm going to go shower and pray that food finally tastes like something other than sand."

"That's horrible."

"Sadly, you get used to it." It was painful, taking a step away from her, leaving her in that room, my room, knowing what I knew.

It was like my soul was getting ripped apart all over again. I'd assumed it would be easy.

I forgot—about free will, about fear.

What a cruel twist of fate, that all would work out in the end, only to find out that the one woman I gave everything up for.

Didn't feel the same way.

CHAPTER TWENTY-THREE

KYRA

I didn't sleep.

Instead, I sat in that room, with my arms hugging my knees to my chest, wondering what was wrong with me.

I'd always been a loner growing up—never really had any friends. Though I tried really hard to connect with people, it always just seemed like people either ignored me or were afraid of me.

My own parents even kept their distance, saying that they just weren't like that.

I remember hugging my mom's leg only to have her give me a sad smile, a pat on the head, then pry my arms from her body.

It stung when I was small.

Who was I kidding? It stung even now.

The worst part was that I had a perfectly gorgeous man—god—rummaging around in the kitchen, and I, Kyra had sent him away.

Sent him away!

I guess he kind of offered but still! Was I insane?

My stomach was in knots, and my chest hurt.

I wanted to believe he was kissing me because he wanted me, yet I couldn't help but think it was because we were destined.

And for once in my life, I wanted someone to just, want *me*, no matter what. No souls, no being reborn, no weird cosmic time travel involved.

Just me.

Maybe I was asking for too much.

Maybe I was just going crazy—at this point, who could really blame me?

"I didn't sacrifice thousands of years of my life for you to pout alone in a bedroom without my brother." Horus's voice stunned me out of my pity party.

I frowned as he braced himself against the door. He was wearing jeans that looked way too tight and a black band T-shirt I'd seen on Tarek once.

"You're back." I gave him a forced smile. "Going into shock yet?"

He shrugged. His dark hair was pulled back into a

ponytail. "I almost got run over by a car. Then again, Mason was driving it, so I've been told that's completely normal. The world is a vastly different place from what it used to be" A wry half-smile tugged up one side of his mouth. "In some ways better, in others much worse." He walked all the way into the room and then sat on the bed. "I expected the door to be locked and the house shaking. Instead I find my brother downstairs grilling a sandwich, whatever that means, and attempting to see if it's possible for a god to get drunk."

I winced. "He tried…"

"Ah, but did you?" Horus fired back. "Did you try or were you afraid?"

I gulped. "It wasn't fear necessarily, more like… okay so it was fear, but he doesn't know me, I mean not really, he can't love me if he doesn't know me."

"Humans." Horus groaned and pressed hand to his temple. "So simple and yet complex. Do you even know what a soul is?"

I narrowed my eyes. "Yes, it's the essence of every person, the only thing that lives, I hope, beyond death."

"Correct, and Anubis, in all his years would weigh souls in the palm of his hand, he would test them, bargain with them, keep them safe, he was the Keeper of Souls. At death, he would weigh a feather against a person's heart and soul and see what won out. He has touched millions of souls. To touch one is to know that person intimately. Imagine the cost on your sanity, imagine the burden he bears. It's not like every soul he touches is good, and yet he takes that in."

My mouth went dry. "Isn't that dangerous?"

"He was made for it," Horus said simply. "The gods were

made in a similar way to humans, given dominion, given souls, and each of us has our job, the one thing that we were told was to never fall as the Watchers did—never involve ourselves with the human races, specifically females."

"That's a lonely existence."

"Absolutely," Horus agreed. "And then you came along, a human with the essence of a god in her blood, the soul of a god in her body, not only did he touch your soul and recognize that you were his other half—but he could actually have you."

"Except I was promised to someone else"

"Exactly. He was willing to die in order to have you, even if it meant his time would suddenly be limited, even if it meant he would be struck down for interfering. He was willing to give up everything for you—and did. The moral of the story is this: What have you sacrificed for Anubis? What have you given him other than his life back? You have given him your trust, you have even given him part of your heart, but you have held the one thing he wants more than anything and hidden it away."

I frowned. "He wants my soul?"

Horus sighed in impatience. "He wants you, his other half, you and only you, Kyra. He could take your soul if he wanted, he could take your very life, he could force you to love him, yet he doesn't. He wants you. And he's eating a sandwich, do you understand me?"

I nodded. "Maybe he likes sandwiches better."

Horus laughed. "Nobody likes food better than sex, least of all a god who's been celibate as long as he has."

My ears perked up. "I'm sorry, what?"

Horus frowned. "Were you listening at all?"

"Yes, and I'm pretty sure you never mentioned that."

"Save me from humans," He put his hands on his hips. "Regardless of the ridiculous stories you may have read about, gods don't just run around creating demigods. Like I said, we have rules. Your other half will always have the blood of the gods running through their bodies meaning you can mate with them—anything outside of that, we don't touch."

"Oh."

"Your cheeks are turning red."

I glared.

Horus just grinned. "I'm off to watch TV, Mason said it's the only way for me to get caught up, though he was going on and on about Lion King—"

"No." I held up my hand. "Log onto Netflix and—"

"Log? You have logs in the house?"

"Er, no, just…" I sighed. "I'll help set you up."

And that was the story of how I helped a god binge watch *Orange is the New Black*. What can I say? He was invested after one episode. I left him in Timber's study and made my way into the kitchen.

A bottle of wine was opened.

A half-eaten sandwich next to it, but no Timber to be found.

Frowning, I went back to the master bedroom and heard the shower. I was just about to leave the room when Timber walked out in nothing but a white towel.

My eyes widened.

He jerked to a stop, water dripping from his hair down his body, his eyes flashing gold while I drank my fill of his perfect muscle tone. Even his feet were sexy—how was that fair?

"Sorry," I blurted. "I didn't know that you were showering."

"I felt dirty." He shrugged and then winced. "That came out wrong."

"Or right," I offered. "However you want to look at it."

The corners of his mouth moved into a dazzling smile. "I thought you were going to nap."

"Yeah, well, your brother needs to catch up on a few thousand years of history so I turned on Netflix for him."

Timber rolled his eyes. "And you thought that was a good idea because?"

"Because, he needs to learn, and watching TV is probably better than taking a stroll downtown and pointing out things while people take pictures of him and weep with ecstasy."

Timber stiffened. "Excuse me?"

"You know…" I waved my hands in front of him. "You guys don't really blend in."

"I blend in just fine." Timber actually looked offended.

I laughed. "Um, no you really don't."

"Do."

"Don't!"

"Do!" He threw his hands up. "I'm the same person!"

"Really?" I grinned. "Care to prove that?"

"Of course."

"Good." I crossed my arms. "Because we're headed to Soul."

His eyes narrowed. "And when I win and everyone recognizes me and nobody runs away screaming or worse, starts humping my leg, what do I get?"

I licked my lips and answered. "Me. You get me."

"And if I lose?" He took a cautious step toward me. "Do I lose you too?"

"No, you just have to sleep on the couch while I take your glorious bed." I winked.

"I feel like I'm being tricked."

"I would never trick a god." I held up my hand. "Scout's honor."

He chuckled. "Little yet absolutely terrifying. Remind me why we hired you again?"

"Oh, you didn't. Tarek did."

That earned me a grunt. "Fine, I can't sleep anyway, may as well check in… maybe I'll get lucky and the girl of my dreams will buy me a drink."

Heat bloomed across my face. "Maybe she will."

"Let's just hope she remembers what I like."

"How could I forget?" I licked my lips.

And then I stood there like an idiot, my body pulsing with the need to be next to his.

"I need to change." He grinned. "You're more than welcome to watch if you think you can handle it."

"Oh!" Flames licked at my already hot face. "No, no, I mean, I'll give you some privacy and just," I almost ran into the door in an effort to escape and felt his laugh like a direct arrow to my heart as I smiled the entire way down the hall.

Progress.

We were making progress.

CHAPTER TWENTY-FOUR

TIMBER

I made her laugh.

Bonus, she didn't shy away from me.

Double bonus, she looked ready to lick me from head to toe.

And on top of that, she talked the entire way to Soul, about the trip to the past, about meeting Ra. I already respected her but hearing the story from her lips did something to me.

She'd risked her life for me.

When we were finally at Soul, I got out of the car and

opened her side helping her out and pressing a hand to the small of her back as we made our way to the entrance.

I knew something was off the minute my security did a double take.

It was late, around one a.m., so I knew the place would be crawling with demons feeding on humans. What I didn't expect was to garner so much attention myself.

Tarek was behind the bar pouring drinks, and Kyra was like a statue next to me as all of the demons stopped feeding and dancing and turned their attention to me.

The music stopped.

It was like a bad movie.

I had no idea what to do.

I was still the Demon King. I had always lorded the underworld and kept that title even when I lost my soul.

But this was different.

This was fear. I could smell it, taste it like ash burning on my tongue.

They were petrified of me.

"So…" Kyra said with fake enthusiasm. "I think we should just act normal and go sit at the bar."

"I am acting normal."

"You're glowing," she said through clenched teeth.

"Shit." The humans were hopefully too drugged to notice. I snapped my fingers at the vamps holding court at the door. Security would need to make sure all the humans' memories were wiped so they didn't report me to CNN. "All right, let's go sit."

Tarek slid two glasses of amber liquid toward us the minute we got to the bar. "So, that's a neat trick, glowing like a Christmas tree. I think a demon shit himself and then puked for good measure."

I sighed. "I didn't realize."

"Timber, you control shadows, darkness, death itself. You could take every remaining soul in this room with the snap of your fingers, send them to Heaven or Hell, you were given that job. Before, you were just creepy as hell and semi-powerful in your own right. Now, well, now you look like you could incinerate everyone with laser eyes."

"Thanks, Tarek," Kyra said through clenched teeth. "Super helpful!"

Tarek looked at her then back at me. "Well, things just took a turn for the worse. What the hell have you guys been doing? Painting each other's nails?"

"Excuse me?" My voice boomed, a few demon shrieks followed. This would take getting used to.

"You..." Tarek pointed at me, "...are fully restored. She..." He pointed at Kyra. "...is still confused and the only way to un-confuse her is to..." He made an odd motion with his hands.

"Are you clapping?" I wondered out loud while Kyra gaped at him.

"Yes. No." Tarek took a deep breath. "You..." More pointing, "...and you..." Repeated pointing. "Are two halves to a whole. You can't be whole unless you're..." He said it slowly, probably for my benefit. "*Who-o-ole.*"

"You're talk in riddles." I grabbed for the glass only to have him get there faster and replace it with something else. "Hey, I was going to drink that!"

"Nope, you both get this now. By the way, I'm not sorry."

He slid two new glasses in front of us. "Now, drink, and be… not too loud."

"You're being weird." Kyra felt his forehead. "Are you sick? Drunk? Sad?"

He slapped her hand away. "No, I'm just frustrated. We risked everything for you two, and you're at happy hour!"

"And that's bad?" Kyra guessed.

Tarek looked ready to murder both of us. "I have customers, deal with this—now—or I'm tattling, and the last thing you need is Dad giving you the sex talk."

Kyra looked absolutely horrified at the thought. Fantastic. Talk of me and her having sex made her look ready to run in front of oncoming traffic.

Cheers!

"The last thing this world needs is Cassius uttering the word sex, to you, in front of him," He pointed to Timber. "It doesn't get more awkward, Alex says he uses sock puppets."

Kyra burst out laughing. "I doubt it."

"Just the idea of it makes me want to break out in hives," Tarek muttered. "Now, finish your drinks and go to the office."

"The office?" I grinned. "Why would we go to the—"

Tarek shrugged while I stood and steadied myself by the bar.

"You okay?" Kyra asked, her eyes dilated, and then she reached out and grabbed my free hand. "Ohhh… You feel *soo* good."

"Your skin always feels like velvet to me."

Her eyes grew hooded. "I can feel your heartbeat."

"Office." Tarek coughed. "Go. Now. I poured you strong

drinks, enough to make you loosen up a bit, but the catch is this—your body sings to him and his to you, alcohol around you two? It's like dousing a fire with kerosene, have fun kids! Off you go!"

"Great idea." I was ready to haul her over my shoulder as we quickly abandoned Tarek and sprinted toward my office.

I barely got the door closed, the lock turned, when Kyra was on me, her fingers digging at my shirt, jerking it open as buttons went flying.

I groaned as I dipped my head and tasted her mouth, the whiskey on her tongue. Her soul shivered in her chest, mine copied.

This.

This was what we needed.

Each other, always each other.

I knew that. She knew that.

And suddenly there was no hesitation, maybe she just needed permission—I would love her forever.

Our tongues twisted together, our mouths sliding in a way that had me kissing down her neck and back up again as her nails dug into my skin. I threw my shirt to the floor and reached for hers.

We were a tangle of arms and legs, kisses, and heat.

I picked her up into my arms and set her on my desk. "You're so beautiful."

"So are you." She wrapped her arms around my neck. I could taste her heartbeat through her kiss, could feel the way it beat for me, strained for me in a way that was other worldly.

"Anubis…" She rasped my name. Mine!

The room shook, it transported me to a different time and place, to a hallway where I grabbed her dress and made her mine, feet from where my father slept.

"Yes." With one hand, I jerked her jeans and underwear down tossing them to the floor as her head fell back, exposing her neck.

Visions flashed before my eyes.

Our hands joined as I deepened the kiss, spread her mouth wider with my tongue, drinking her while her soul chanted my name.

Thunder cracked in the distance as papers crashed to the floor followed by the phone.

I didn't care.

I panted against her body, then spread her legs wide, my fingers digging into the sensitive skin of her thighs, I was delirious from her taste, from the way she clung to me like I was her everything.

"Kyra, I need you. I've always…" My voice deepened, took on a gravelly tone. "…needed you."

"I've always been yours." She bit down on my bottom lip and then bruised me with her kiss, her fingers dancing along my skin, driving me crazy, I couldn't remember a time ever being so aroused.

"You are mine, Kyra, daughter of Apollo."

"Yes." She panted. "Yesss."

I was out of control, almost feral as I gripped her hips and jerked her body closer. I was inside her in seconds.

One.

No longer a half.

A whole.

The sound of lightning cracking split through the room as I surged forward, unable to slow my thrusts or the screams of pleasure as darkness filled my line of vision.

Thousands of years.

I would wait more.

Yet for this. I would wait an eternity.

My soul wept and then it was like being reborn, soul touching soul, hearts aligned, and bodies in perfect sync as I gripped her hips.

Kyra's eyes opened, and what I saw there was perfection.

Golden. Perfection.

Because I was a part of her now, forever.

Her lips parted as she found her release, and I followed, not realizing that there was more to our story.

Not realizing, until in a haze of sex we looked around the room… and found every single object incinerated to dust.

CHAPTER
TWENTY-FIVE

KYRA

Egypt, Valley of the gods

"*I don't understand.*" *My father was speaking, but surely I was misunderstanding what he was trying to convey.* "*Why would you do this to me?*"

"*I'm protecting you.*" *He wiped a tear.* "*The only way I know how.*"

"*By taking everything from me?*" *My hands shook.* "*You're taking a gift that was given, you're taking all the parts of you that I love, that make me yours!"*

"The Creator is all knowing." My father hung his head. "He gave me two choices. Take the essence of the gods that flow through your veins while your soul remains intact, or you'll be used for evil. I can't allow that, you are the daughter of Apollo! The granddaughter of Ra himself! A weapon I cannot allow in the wrong hands!"

"But—" Tears stung. I felt betrayed. "How do we know the worst is going to happen?"

"The worst," My father paled. "Is yet to come. Don't you see it? The gods are a dying race. Even now, they give in to their baser instincts! And you, you are the only one who can help them sustain this life, you are life itself, you house the sun!"

I smiled sadly. "A gift."

He nodded. "One I am taking back until the right time."

"How will I know?"

"Trials and tribulations." My grandfather joined us in all his shining glory. "We have served the Creator for centuries and he has served us as well. If he says this is what we must do, we do it."

My hands shook as I held them out.

It didn't take long.

My skin was gold and then everything felt lifeless, cold.

"I'm sorry." My father wept as he pulled immortality from my veins. It was like watching my identity get stolen in front of my very eyes as the shimmery gold blood from the gods was pulled from my skin in a thick mist. It burned from the inside out. I wasn't sure what was worse the pain or the knowledge that I was no longer myself. When he was done, he pressed it into a necklace shaped like the sun and handed it to my grandfather.

It pulsed as he wrapped it around my neck.

"One day…" Grandfather winked. "You will thank us, I only hope we are around to see that love shine in your eyes. You won't walk this earth alone, for your soul is matched with another. His strength will sustain you until the right time. He will awaken you in ways you cannot imagine. You will both suffer horrible tragedies, but you will one day be whole. Praise be to the Creator, let that day be swift in its coming."

"He is fair." My father nodded. "I promise you this." He smiled brightly. "Your journey will one day have an ending that turns into a marvelous beginning. Consider yourself blessed, daughter of Apollo, Keeper of Light. Balance to the dark."

Grandfather kissed his thumb and forefinger then pressed them against my forehead and whispered. "Amen."

Present Day

I gasped. Timber stared at me with a blinding smile, and then he pressed a gentle kiss to my forehead. "Doing some time travel or just remembering?"

"Remembering." My throat hurt, tears burned my eyes. "I knew he took the essence of the gods from me, I just wasn't sure why. I though he wanted me to live a normal life. Instead, they were told someone would use me."

Timber stiffened. "Set."

"Yes." I knew it in my soul in the twisted way he looked at me. "I could have restored his power."

"How?" Timber frowned.

I reached for my ever-present necklace, touched it with my fingertips. "Because I house the sun."

Timber grabbed the necklace and jerked it from my neck. Then, without asking permission or even speaking, he pressed it between two fingers, crushing it into dust and blowing it into my face.

I sucked in a sharp breath as searing heat enveloped me.

It burned down my fingertips, made me feel simultaneously hot and cold.

"Welcome back." Timber grinned. "Daughter of Apollo."

CHAPTER
TWENTY-SIX

TIMBER

"So everything just went... poof?" Mason motioned with his hands while Serenity started pouring wine. The sound of kids playing was like a balm to my soul—again I'd take that to my grave.

The love I felt for the wives.

For their children.

I would protect them with my dying breath.

We'd only just gotten back to Ethan's house. I wasn't sure

why everything was incinerated, and even though I knew I would catch shit for a lifetime—I told them what happened.

"Yes." I shrugged. "Everything turned to ash."

Alex held his hand up for a high five, earning an eye roll from Mason and a middle finger from Tarek.

Ethan and Cassius paced in the kitchen while Kyra played with the twins, making faces, and holding them, listening to Genesis telling her stories about demon bites.

Perfect.

I wanted to remind her… *that* part of me was gone, but she seemed interested, and dare I say aroused? Hmm, might revisit that.

"He's glowing again." This from an annoyed Alex.

I rolled my eyes. "Look, I know you have Ra's essence in you, I'm sure you're related and just omitted that part of the story, but look at her." I pointed to Kyra, "She has more than you do."

"She's a pure blood." Mason popped a berry into his mouth. "What?" Another shrug. "She's the daughter of Apollo, the granddaughter of Ra, it's not hard math. The only troubling thing is the fact that she can be drained… used."

Even now, Kyra was glowing just like I was. It was more subtle, prettier, almost like something shiny you want to keep for yourself. No wonder Apollo did what he did; he was protecting her, not cursing her.

"Thanks for that," I said dryly. "As always, Mason, so helpful."

Tarek grinned from his side of the room. "You emptied the place, I'm impressed."

I glared. "Tell me you listened and I'm murdering you, dog."

"I would never!" He winked. "But I did take advantage of the fact that both of you needed more than one shot of alcohol and didn't realize that just being around each other would make it happen within seconds, when you have your soulmate your body can't say no. It's a thing. You're welcome!"

I narrowed my eyes. "You're a hazard to my health."

Tarek sniffed.

Ethan paused, "Is he crying now?"

"I like to be useful!" Tarek shrugged.

Immortals, can't live with them, can't live without them.

Cassius smiled, and then in an instant the smile was gone as he grabbed his wife by the arm and gently squeezed.

"Stephanie." His eyes went an icy white; the room dropped a solid fifty degrees. "Take the kids upstairs immediately. Genesis, stay with them. We'll need Serenity. And guard Hope with your life, Genesis, understand me? Nothing happens to the last elf we have on this plane!"

"Yes." In a blink Genesis was gone with Hope, Stephanie, and the kids. Serenity stayed behind, I imagined, because she was part goddess and was in this just as much as we were.

A hot wind picked up lessening the chill.

More angels?

Enemies?

The house shook beneath my feet.

And there, in an instant, stood my father, Set, at about the same time Horus came barreling into the room. "He's coming!"

"*He's...*" My father tilted his head in glee and spread his arms wide. "...already here."

CHAPTER TWENTY-SEVEN

KYRA

I'd known fear several times in my life. When my parents left, when I realized that I wouldn't have lasting relationships in this world, when I'd wake up in a cold sweat from dreams that seemed so real I could still smell the fragrance of flowers in the air.

This was a different sort of fear.

One that told me I wouldn't survive.

One that told me this man in front of me was out for

blood and would win regardless of how much we tried to stop him.

Set's eyes had gone completely black which meant only one thing: his soul was dying. I wondered how much this had cost him, traveling into this space in time. I wondered what he had sacrificed in order to do it.

In order to use me.

The memories that had been fuzzy were now clear as day. My love for Timber, as weird as it seemed wasn't weird at all, but a tethered connection, like an invisible rope between us that made me feel like I belonged.

He immediately shoved me behind him.

I loved him for that.

For being willing to put his life on the line every single time. I think that was what I had noticed about him first, his supreme control, his desire to do right over wrong every single time even if he suffered for it.

And then I had fallen for the way he cracked a smile when I pushed him too far. We'd had sixty days of love together, not just sex but love, laughter, talked of a family even though we knew it would be impossible to bring a child into a world we wouldn't be a part of anymore.

And I remembered that night, being absolutely terrified, when he gave me one last kiss.

"I'll love you forever." The gold from his eyes had left, they were so black and flashed red scaring me to death as he closed them and before my very eyes grew two horns on his head.

"I did this to you." I wept against his chest. "Our love did this!"

"No!" He roared his fangs descending like he couldn't control them. "Our love didn't destroy anything. We chose love, and Set chose to punish us because of it. Don't worry." He winced like something was breaking inside his chest.

I thought it was his heart, since mine was breaking too.

I thought wrong, as his soul slithered from his body in one last attempt to touch mine.

I reached out and grabbed it in my fingertips and watched his god-like soul die in the palm of my hand, turning to the black of ash.

And when I looked up, the Anubis I knew was gone.

A red tear slid down his cheek as his father slapped him across the face. "You don't deserve the name of the gods!" Another slap. "From here on out, you will be known as nothing but Timber that burns day in and day out without ever truly disappearing, you are nothing but wood that refuses to burn out, and every damn time you wish for death, I'll remind you of what you are! A Demon King from Hell!"

Timber fell to his knees and raged while I stumbled backward.

"As for you," Set rasped. "Daughter of Apollo, I no longer have any use for you. But I curse you to walk this earth in search of the one you love who will never be reborn! I curse you to a continuous life in search for the very soul that died by your hand. And I hope you have nightmares of this life over and over again, knowing that in the end you could have been a queen! Instead, you're nothing but a human with a good bloodline. I rebuke you in the name of the Creator!"

"Not so fast." Ra appeared. "It is true, there are consequences to every action, but as her grandfather, I choose to offer a gift."

Set glared. "Give your gift and be gone from my temple!"

"One day," Ra pressed a searing hand to my cheek. "You will wake up and the world will not be filled with monsters. One day, you will find what your soul searches for. One day, a race will be restored, and he will make another choice that will set about something so wonderful your heart won't be able to contain it. I will make it so."

Set grumbled. "Only the Creator can make such a promise."

"I know." Ra smiled brightly. "Chin up, dear girl. Love is the strongest gift we are given! And it is now my love, my unconditional love for you, that gives you this gift." He closed his eyes, and in a flash, I saw the very essence of the sun leave his body in tiny particles that lifted toward the heavens. "I sacrifice my life so that you have your future."

"No!" Set roared. "She must be punished!"

Ra ignored him, and in a flash, his body collapsed against the marble steps.

A warm wind picked up as the sound of trumpets filled the air, so piercing I covered my ears.

At least three thousand angels descended, all wearing black armor, helmets so huge it would fit three of Set's heads inside them, and in the very middle, a boy.

The small boy smiled at me and nodded toward two angels who very gently picked up my grandfather's body and brought it to the middle of the circle.

"It is done." The boy's voice shook the earth beneath my feet. "Live well, daughter of Apollo—remember who you are, remember what you were created for—sacrificed for—life!"

I stumbled against Timber as the memory left and turned my attention toward Set.

I wasn't sure how long I had been lost in the memory.

All I knew was that we didn't have much time, and that Set was weak.

"You cannot have her." Timber glared.

Set eyed him up and down. "Son, you've grown."

"I am no longer your son. I am Anubis, Prince of Darkness, and you will bow in the presence of royalty!"

I almost cheered at the furious look on Set's face. "I will always be more powerful than you."

"You stink of sin," Timber clipped. "After all, I would know, I'm the darkest sinner of them all. I roamed the earth for centuries, I killed, I destroyed, I fought wars in the name of the demon race. The earth was filled with blood from my hands. Believe me when I say, like recognizes like."

Set ground his teeth. "It cost me everything to get here—to take back—" He pointed at me. "—what you stole!"

"You're too late," I said in a calm voice. "I'm already his."

"You were promised to me!" Set roared. Black blood began oozing from his mouth.

Timber's hand reached for mine. Energy surged between us.

Cassius took a tentative step toward Set. "The time of the gods is long passed, King Set. Even here, you feel your power dwindle, the Creator limits it during this time. It's why you feel sick. You are weaker than a fly, and you are standing in a room full of the most powerful immortals in the known world. Do you truly think you stand a chance?"

"All I need is one chance." Set's red eyes flashed toward me. "All I need is her, and I can destroy each and every one of you." His voice smoothed, grew cunning. "I wonder what you value most, the children upstairs? Or your wives?"

"That's it." Ethan's fangs descended. "I'm killing him right the hell now."

"Get in line." Mason's eyes flashed white.

Horus tightened his hands into fists as he moved closer, ready to pounce. I reached for my necklace only realizing that it was gone when I touched skin.

It was in me.

Timber had put Ra's essence back inside me where it belonged.

Together, we were dark and light.

Both were good, both were powerful.

I smiled at Set. "I'll go with you under one condition."

"You'll stay right the hell there!" Timber growled.

I was made for this moment.

Ra had died for this moment.

My grandfather, my family.

He was dead.

But I wondered in that moment, if someone else was alive. We had ancient gods in that room.

The more of us, the more powerful, right?

I closed my eyes and fell to my knees. "Creator, my Father, I ask for you to deliver my father and my mother."

Set laughed.

I didn't.

Because in a blinding blaze of white light, both my parents appeared wearing the same old weird clothes they always did.

"So..." My father nodded to Cassius. "It has come to this."

"It has." Cassius answered.

"Well." My mom winked at me. "It has been a very long time."

I frowned. They were my parents from this era, the twenty-first century, and they looked at me like they were powerful enough to do something instead of throw a punch and run in the opposite direction.

"The gods," my father said in a voice that shook the house. "Do not intervene. I'm sorry, Kyra, we could only lead you in the right direction century after century. When you continued to be reborn we tried… We almost lost hope."

I shook my head. "I don't understand."

"We've been here the entire time, the entire journey, Ra's last gift wasn't just a sacrifice for you—it was for our family."

My mom turned her attention to Set. "You don't seem well. Rough journey?"

Set heaved. The black ooze left his mouth in a thick stream.

My father casually walked over to me and grabbed my hand then nodded to Timber. "I knew you'd find each other."

Timber smiled and then grabbed my other hand. Slowly and surely every immortal in that room had joined hands against Set. Their power surged as the house shook. A dark mist started filling up the room as the light from the rest of us blinded Set's face. He crumpled to the ground, screaming in agony. Alex was glowing orange and red while Serenity's eyes had gone a scary looking blue.

Set gripped his throat with both hands as sores appeared up and down his arms. At this point, I wasn't sure who was doing what, just that he was getting quickly stripped of everything that made him a god.

More ash and smoke wrapped itself around Set's feet, pulling him into the floor like he was getting drawn into the depths of Hell or maybe being trapped between two planes for an eternity.

Timber jerked him back to his feet and slammed his fist into his chest, pulling his still beating heart from his body as he held it in his hand.

"Cassius," Timber growled. "A feather, if you don't mind."

"No!" Set screamed. "You can't!"

"My pleasure." Cassius chuckled and handed Timber one purple feather.

"King Set..." Timber's body shook and then morphed into the jackal, all sleek black fur, pointy ears and nose. "The truth of your heart is black. I condemn you to death."

"I am a god!" He wailed in pain as something lifted from the dark mist.

A woman in all black with razor sharp teeth, green skin, and red hair. "Anubis, it has been an age." She winked.

"Mania." He nodded. "I brought you a snack."

"Like I said..." Mania grinned seductively at Set. "I knew I would be entertained when I gave you that borrowed soul. Worth every penny." She pressed a claw against Set's head. "You ready for a feast, King Set? Because I've been watching you for centuries."

"No." Set shrieked. "No!"

"Be gone, goddess of death," Cassius snapped. "And take your pathetic snack with you."

"Angels," she huffed. "So demanding. Do put in a good word upstairs."

With that, the dark mist consumed them both leaving nothing but a mark of ash where they stood and a black stone heart in Timber's hand.

I exhaled in relief and threw my arms around his neck. "You did it!"

"Who knew I'd grow up and become a team player?" Timber shrugged.

"Literally none of us." Alex yawned. "Literally."

"Alex." My father went over to him and patted him on the shoulder. "I'm curious, how did you find your travels?"

"Boring." Alex grinned and then shrugged. "Kidding, I was quite entertained by Kyra here and the way she spoke to Set, though it nearly got us killed it was worth it, because now dipshit's back, yay!"

He was pointing at Timber, who just rolled his eyes and held me close.

Horus slumped against one of the barstools. "Tell me every Tuesday night isn't always like this."

Complete silence and then…

"Never!"

"Totally boring."

"We garden!"

"Look, my tomatoes are coming in." Mason started moving to the window while a quiet Tarek sat town next to Horus and grinned.

Horus narrowed his eyes. "Why are you looking at me like that? Why is he looking at me like that?"

"He likes to make friends." Timber laughed. "He's *your* problem now, brother."

"I'll grow on you." Tarek slapped him on the back. "Plus I see some very interesting times in your future, Prince of Light. How do you feel about cougars?"

"The animal?"

"The woman." Tarek nodded slowly. "You better bring your A game. She's feisty."

"Fantastic, just what I wanted," Horus said dryly. "Feisty."

I turned in Timber's arms and pressed a kiss to his mouth. "Worth it, it was worth it, wasn't it?"

"Yes." His eyes glowed a warm gold. "It was."

I suddenly didn't want to be in that room anymore, or anywhere near other people. I was already imagining clawing his clothes from his body.

He growled low in his throat and pulled me against his chest, kissing me soundly. "Bathroom."

"But I don't have to—ohhhh, yes, bathroom, now, to er, clean up the…" We both eyed the black heart still in his hands. "Ash?"

"Let's just go with ash," he agreed as we snuck away from everyone, even though they had to know what was happening. My own father blushed and looked away.

I didn't care.

He was mine.

I was his.

And our moment had finally arrived.

After centuries of searching.

Our journey had led us home.

CHAPTER TWENTY-EIGHT

TIMBER

I locked the bathroom door and immediately pulled every stitch of clothing off of her and tossed it to the floor. Her skin was positively glowing. Her smile was an addiction I could get used to as I nipped her lips and held her body close, just needing a few minutes with her, a few minutes to hold her there, frozen in time while the reality of what had just happened settled over us.

"I have searched for you for thousands of years," I rasped, my voice heavy with emotion. "Don't make me wait any longer to be inside you again, to feel your legs wrapped around me. I don't think I could survive it."

"That," Kyra said, pulling my shirt over my head, "makes two of us."

Our mouths collided as she pulled open the button to my jeans, freeing me.

I hooked her legs around my waist, grabbing her at the knees to angle deeper. "One day there will be a bed."

Her head fell back against the glass as she laughed. "As long as I have you, I don't really care."

"Good answer." I slid my mouth across hers and bit down on her lower lip, swirling my tongue across the swollen pieces of skin that I couldn't stop sucking and tasting.

"Now, Anubis."

"You keep calling me that." I didn't admit that I liked it more.

"Because…" Her eyes flashed gold. "In this world, Timber was my boss, my friend, the demon who protected me even though he had no reason to. But Anubis? He's the other half of my soul. And since you're one person I figured, in this moment, when I'm baring body and soul to you—you deserve to be called, not Timber, but my Anubis, Prince of Darkness, Keeper of Souls—mine!"

"Say it!" I thrust into her, slamming my hand against the glass behind her head as it cracked beneath my fingertips. "Say it again!'

"Anubis, Keeper of Souls." She panted in my arms as I strained to keep focus. "Mine."

"Yes!" I growled as our bodies slammed together and hit the glass again and again until nothing but shards remained around our feet. "Seeing your pleasure is everything to me, holding you—even better."

"Mmm," She drew a small circle around my chest and then a tiny blue tentacle reached out and grabbed her finger. "I think you like me."

"No. I love you. With every part of me."

Tears filled her eyes. "I'm so sorry for not trusting you, for not remembering."

"Shhh." I cupped her chin with both hands and winked. "At least now we have time."

"No. No you don't," Ethan growled from the other side of the door. "If you break anything, I swear I'll—"

I snapped my fingers as a dark mist curled beneath the door.

"Son of a bitch, Timber! Why am I seeing my worst nightmare come to life? Horus! Horus!"

I shrugged and kissed Kyra again.

"We owe him a mirror," she pointed out.

"He's rich, he'll be okay." I sighed in contentment. "But if it makes you happy, we'll go to Home Depot and find him a stupid mirror. Damn vampire likes to look at himself too much."

She laughed as I slowly helped her put her clothes back on. Kyra was just reaching for my jeans when she gave me her back and turned on the shower, then looked over her shoulder. "Can't break much in here."

I took her word for it.

Our bill at Home Depot was twelve hundred dollars.

And as I handed over my card, all I kept thinking was... *worth it.*

Worth it all.

"How do you feel about kids?" She asked as we climbed into my Maserati.

"I think they better have more light than dark or those toddlers are going to be a nightmare." I tried to keep the excitement out of my voice.

And as we drove off, literally toward my house and the sunset, I heard a familiar chuckle.

"So, bloody entertaining, Anubis. I'll be back for your brother."

ABOUT THE AUTHOR

Rachel Van Dyken is the #1 New York Times Bestselling, Wall Street Journal, and USA Today bestselling author of over 80 books ranging from contemporary romance to paranormal. With over four million copies sold, she's been featured in Forbes, US Weekly, and USA Today. Her books have been translated in more than 15 countries. She was one of the first romance authors to have a Kindle in Motion book through Amazon publishing and continues to strive to be on the cutting edge of the reader experience. She keeps her home in the Pacific Northwest with her husband, adorable son, naked cat, and two dogs. For more information about her books and upcoming events, visit www.RachelVanDykenauthor. com.

ALSO BY
RACHEL VAN DYKEN

Kathy Ireland & Rachel Van Dyken
Fashion Jungle

Eagle Elite
Elite
Elect
Entice
Elicit
Bang Bang
Enforce
Ember
Elude

Empire
Enrage
Eulogy
Envy

Elite Bratva Brotherhood
RIP
Debase

The Bet Series
The Bet
The Wager
The Dare

Seaside Series
Tear
Pull
Shatter
Forever
Fall
Strung
Eternal

Seaside Pictures
Capture
Keep
Steal
All Stars Fall
Abandon

Curious Liaisons
Cheater
Cheater's Regret

Players Game
Fraternize
Infraction
M.V.P.

Liars, Inc
Dirty Exes
Dangerous Exes

Cruel Summer
Summer Heat
Summer Seduction
Summer Nights

Waltzing With The Wallflower
Waltzing with the Wallflower
Beguiling Bridget
Taming Wilde

London Fairy Tales
Upon a Midnight Dream
Whispered Music
The Wolf's Pursuit
When Ash Falls

Renwick House

The Ugly Duckling Debutante
The Seduction of Sebastian St. James
The Redemption of Lord Rawlings
An Unlikely Alliance
The Devil Duke Takes a Bride

Other Titles

The Parting Gift
Compromising Kessen
Savage Winter
Divine Uprising
Every Girl Does It
Co-Ed
A Crown for Christmas

CPSIA information can be obtained
at www.ICGtesting.com
Printed in the USA
LVHW031125161019
634268LV00004B/683/P